This book belongs to

Ellie: Dragon lover ♥

TALES OF
DRAGONS
& MONSTERS

Compiled by Tig Thomas

Miles
KeLLy

First published in 2017 by Miles Kelly Publishing Ltd
Harding's Barn, Bardfield End Green, Thaxted, Essex, CM6 3PX, UK

2 4 6 8 10 9 7 5 3 1

Publishing Director Belinda Gallagher
Creative Director Jo Cowan
Editorial Director Rosie Neave
Editor Sarah Parkin
Designer Jo Cowan
Editorial Assistant Amy Johnson
Production Elizabeth Collins, Caroline Kelly
Reprographics Stephan Davis, Jennifer Cozens, Thom Allaway
Assets Lorraine King

ISBN 978-1-78617-322-5

Printed in China

British Library Cataloguing-in-Publication Data
A catalogue record for this book is available from the British Library

ACKNOWLEDGEMENTS

The publishers would like to thank the following artists who have contributed to this book:
Advocate Art Andy Catling, Robert Dunn, Sara Sanchez, Mónica Armiño (cover)
The Bright Agency Gerald Kelley

The publishers would like to thank **Shutterstock.com** for the use of their photographs:
b/g = background, r/t = repeated throughout
Page 1 caesart; 3(r/t) caesart; 4 caesart; 5(banner) Andrea Danti, (b/g)(r/t) AnnPainter, (r/t) Lora liu;
6(r/t) Lukiyanova Natalia/frenta; 7(r/t) caesart; 8(r/t) maximanl; 9(r/t) Kompaniets Taras;
10–11(b/g)(r/t) caesart; 12(r/t) Kompaniets Taras; 24(r/t) sharpner; 31(r/t) Kompaniets Taras;
44(r/t) Apostrophe; 51(r/t) koya979; 64(r/t) sharpner; 71(r/t) Kompaniets Taras; 80(r/t) mmaxer;
90(r/t) AnnPainter; 103(r/t) Apostrophe; 112–113(b/g)(r/t) Lukiyanova Natalia/frenta; 164(r/t) AnnPainter;
174(r/t) Tancha; 208–209(b/g)(r/t) Vilmos Varga; 256(r/t) koya979; 270 caesart; 288(r/t) Tihis;
308–309(b/g)(r/t) Ann_Mei; 310(r/t) Kompaniets Taras

Every effort has been made to acknowledge the source and copyright holder of each picture.
Miles Kelly Publishing apologises for any unintentional errors or omissions.

The majority of stories in this book have been cut and edited for clarity.

Made with paper from a sustainable forest

www.mileskelly.net

Contents

10–111
SCALES AND TAILS

112–207
BOGGARTS, TROLLS AND GOBLINS

208–307
GRUESOME GIANTS AND AWFUL OGRES

308–384
WEIRD AND WONDERFUL BEASTS

SCALES AND TAILS

The Sea-Serpent
E Pauline Johnson
12

Hercules and the Hydra
R E Francillon
24

Philip the Dragon-Slayer
E Nesbit, from a chapter of *The Magic City*
31

Raiko Slays the Demon
William Elliot Griffis
44

Fafnir, the Dragon
James Baldwin, from *The Story of Siegfried*
51

St George and the Dragon
Flora Annie Steel
64

The Laidly Worm
Flora Annie Steel
71

The Mighty Monster Afang
William Elliot Griffis
80

The Quarrelsome Dragons
L Frank Baum, from *The Tin Man of Oz*
90

Perseus and Andromeda
R E Francillon
103

Boggarts, Trolls and Goblins

Farmer Griggs's Boggart   114
Howard Pyle, from *Pepper and Salt*

How an Old Man Lost His Wart   125
A traditional Japanese tale

The Farmer and the Boggart   137
Anon

How the Goblins Turned to Stone   142
William Elliot Griffis

The Christmas Goblins   152
Charles Dickens

The Goblin's Arm   164
William Elliot Griffis

The Troll and the Bear   174
A traditional Norwegian tale

The Nix in Mischief   180
Mrs Ewing

The Widow's Son   190
Katharine Pyle, a Scandinavian tale

The Troll Who Wrote a Letter   202
A traditional Scandinavian tale

Gruesome Giants and Awful Ogres

Giant Ton and Giant Blubb 210
William Elliot Griffis

Buchettino 220
Thomas Frederick Crane

Brabo and the Giant 228
William Elliot Griffis

Odysseus and the Cyclops 236
Andrew Lang

Jack in Wales 248
Flora Annie Steel

The Three Little Pigs and the Ogre 256
Howard Pyle

Thor's Adventures among the Giants 270
Julia Goddard, from *Wonderful Stories from Northern Lands*

Momotaro 282
John Finnemore, a traditional Japanese folk tale

Thirteenth 288
Thomas Frederick Crane

The Giant of the Flood 297
Gertrude Landa

Weird and Wonderful Beasts

John Malin and the Bull-man   310
Katharine Pyle, a Louisiana tale

Perseus and the Gorgon   322
James Baldwin

The Sphinx   334
Anon

The Bogey-Beast   340
Flora Annie Steel

The Red Ettin   349
Joseph Jacobs

The Master and his Pupil   359
Joseph Jacobs

The Cattle of Geryon   366
R E Francillon, from Of Gods and Monsters

Talus, the Brass Giant   378
Charles Kingsley, from The Heroes

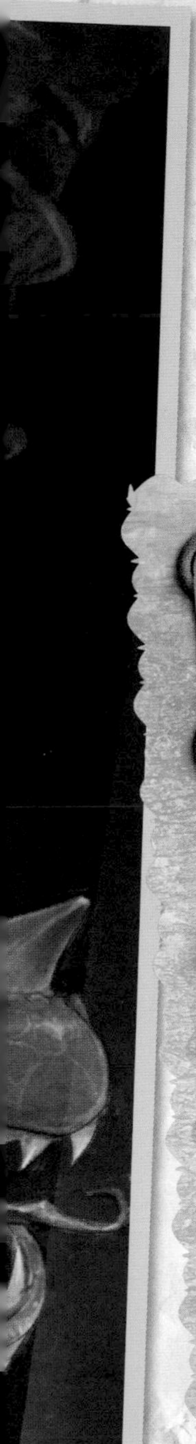

SCALES AND TAILS

The Sea-Serpent   12

Hercules and the Hydra   24

Philip the Dragon-Slayer   31

Raiko Slays the Demon   44

Fafnir, the Dragon   51

St George and the Dragon   64

The Laidly Worm   71

The Mighty Monster Afang   80

The Quarrelsome Dragons   90

Perseus and Andromeda   103

The Sea-Serpent

E Pauline Johnson

This tale is told by an old American Indian. He describes how one of his people became too fond of money, and how God, the Great Spirit, turned him into a terrible monster.

"Yes, it was during the first gold craze, and many of our young men went as guides to the white men far up the river. When the young men returned they brought tales of greed and murder back with them, and our old people and our women shook their heads and said evil would come of it.

"But all our young men, except one, returned as they went – kind to the poor, kind to those who were foodless, sharing whatever they had. But one, who was called Shak-shak (which means 'the Hawk'), came back with hoards of gold nuggets. He was rich like the white men and, like them, he kept it. He would count his money, count his nuggets, gloat over them and toss them in his palms. He loved them better than food, better than his life.

"The entire tribe arose. They said Shak-shak had the disease of greed. To cure it, he must give a great feast, divide his riches with the poorer people, share them with the old, the sick, the foodless. But he jeered and

laughed and told them 'No', and went on loving and gloating over his gold.

"Then the Great Spirit poked out of the sky and said, 'Shak-shak, you will not listen to the cry of the hungry, to the call of the old and sick. You will not share your possessions. You have disobeyed the ancient laws of your people. Now I will make you

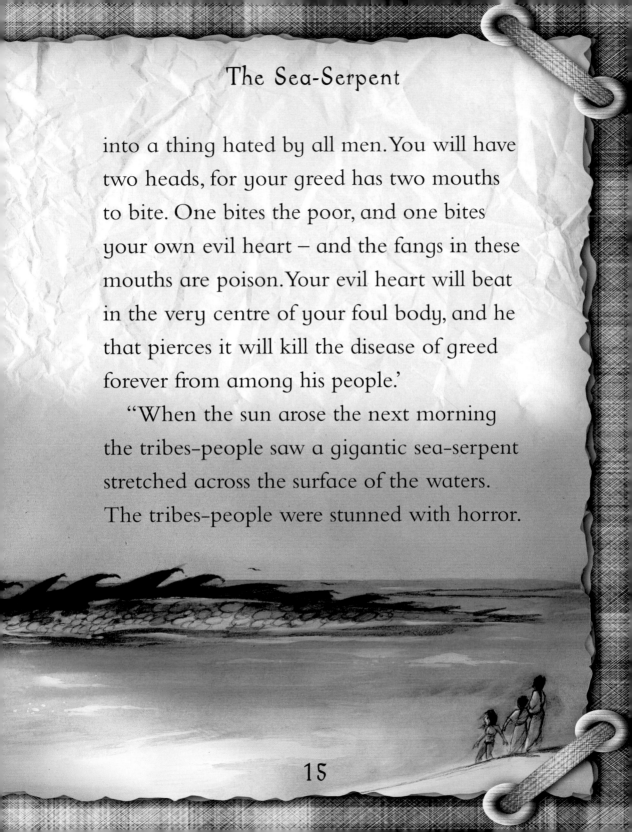

into a thing hated by all men. You will have two heads, for your greed has two mouths to bite. One bites the poor, and one bites your own evil heart – and the fangs in these mouths are poison. Your evil heart will beat in the very centre of your foul body, and he that pierces it will kill the disease of greed forever from among his people.'

"When the sun arose the next morning the tribes-people saw a gigantic sea-serpent stretched across the surface of the waters. The tribes-people were stunned with horror.

Scales and Tails

They loathed the creature, they hated it, they feared it. Day after day it lay there, its monstrous heads lifted out of the waters, its mile-long body blocking all entrance to the sea. The chiefs made council, the medicine men danced and chanted, but the Serpent never moved. After the chiefs and medicine men had done all in their power, and still the Serpent lay across the waters, a handsome boy of sixteen approached them and reminded them of the words of the Great Spirit.

"'Let me try to find this evil heart, oh great men of my tribe,' he cried. 'Let me wage war upon this creature and try to rid my people of this greed.'

"The boy was brave. His tribes-people called him the Tenas Tyee (Little Chief) and

they loved him. He hunted food for the old
people, and he tanned skins and furs for
those whose feet were
feeble and whose
eyes were fading.

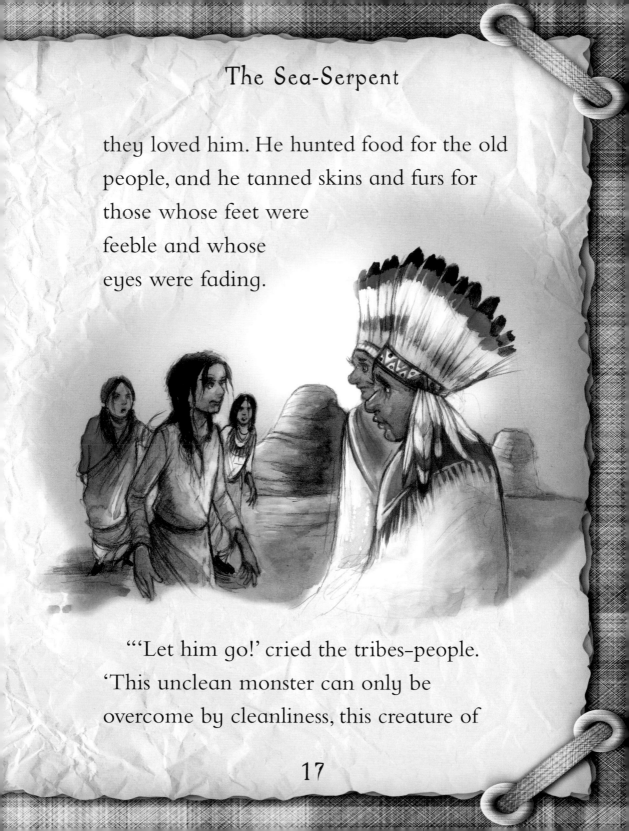

"'Let him go!' cried the tribes-people.
'This unclean monster can only be
overcome by cleanliness, this creature of

greed can only be overthrown by generosity. Let him go!' The chiefs and the medicine men listened, then agreed. 'Go,' they commanded, 'and fight this monster with your strongest weapons – cleanliness and generosity.'

"The Tenas Tyee turned to his mother. 'I shall be gone four days,' he told her, 'and I shall swim all that time. I have tried all my life to be generous, but the people say I must be clean also to fight this unclean creature. While I am gone put fresh furs on my bed every day, even if I am not here to lie on them. If I know my bed, my body and my heart are all clean I can overcome this serpent.'

"'Your bed shall have fresh furs every morning,' his mother said simply.

The Sea-Serpent

"The Tenas Tyee then stripped himself and, with no clothing except a belt into which he thrust his hunting knife, he flung his young body into the sea.

"But at the end of four days he did not return. Sometimes his people could see him swimming far out in mid-channel, trying to find the exact centre of the Serpent, where lay its evil, selfish heart. But on the fifth morning they saw him rise out of the sea and greet the rising sun with outstretched arms.

"Weeks and months went by, and still the Tenas Tyee would swim daily searching for that heart of greed. Each morning the sunrise glinted on his body as he stood with outstretched arms greeting the coming day and then plunging from the

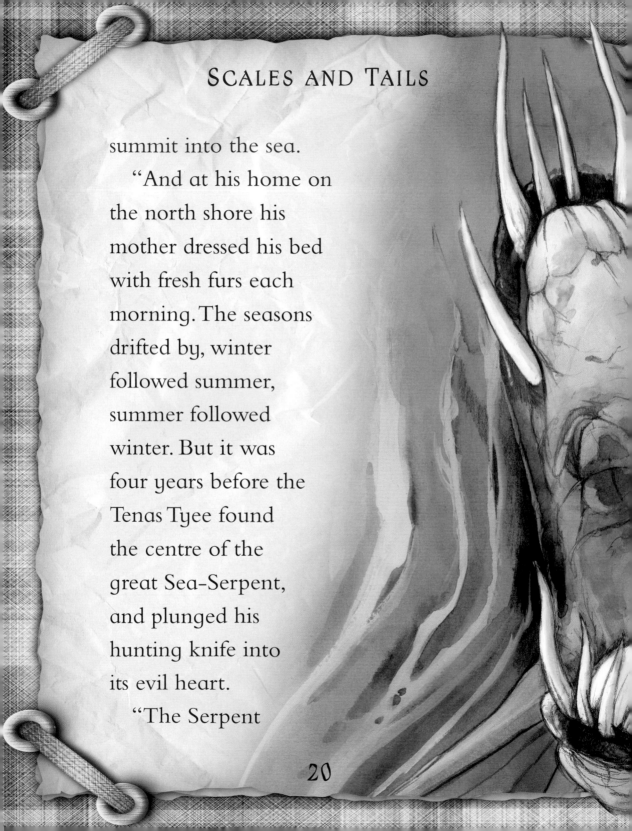

summit into the sea.

"And at his home on the north shore his mother dressed his bed with fresh furs each morning. The seasons drifted by, winter followed summer, summer followed winter. But it was four years before the Tenas Tyee found the centre of the great Sea-Serpent, and plunged his hunting knife into its evil heart.

"The Serpent

The Sea-Serpent

writhed, leaving a trail of blackness on the water. Its huge body began to shrink and shrivel. It became dwarfed and withered, until nothing but the bones of its back remained, and they, sea-bleached and lifeless, soon sank to the bed of the ocean. But as the Tenas Tyee swam homeward and his clean body crossed through the black stain left by the Serpent, the waters became clear and blue and sparkling. He had overcome even the trail of the Serpent.

"When at last the Tenas Tyee stood in the doorway of his home, he said, 'My mother, I could not have killed the monster of greed among my people had you not helped me by keeping one place for me at home fresh and clean for my return.'

"She looked at him as only mothers look.

'Each day these four years, I have laid fresh furs on your bed. Sleep now and rest, oh my Tenas Tyee,' she said."

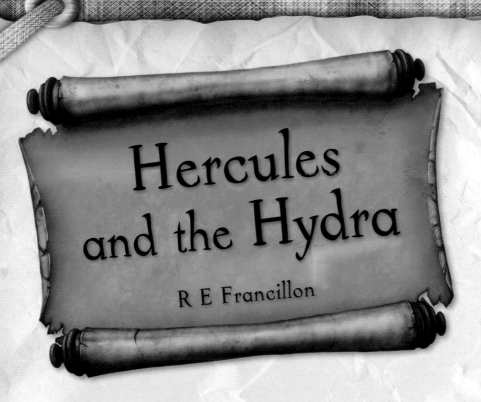

Hercules and the Hydra

R E Francillon

Hercules has been given the task of performing twelve labours by King Eurystheus. The second of these labours is to kill the terrible twelve-headed monster, the Hydra.

The Hydra was a huge water-snake, which lived in Lake Lerna, from where it used to go forth to find humans to eat. It had a hundred heads, and from each of its hundred mouths darted a forked tongue of flame, dripping with poison.

Hercules and the Hydra

Hercules set forth for Lake Lerna. But he did not go to work without making plans and taking all the precautions he could think of. He remembered the thickness and toughness of the Nemaean lion's skin, which he had just killed, so he had it made into a sort of cloak, which served him for armour better than brass or steel. He also made a young oak-tree into a regular club, which became his favourite weapon. And instead of going alone, he took with him his friend and cousin, Iolas, to act as his squire. You can always know Hercules in pictures and statues by his knotted club and his lion-skin.

It was easy enough to find the Hydra – only too easy. It had its nest in a foul swamp, the air of which its breath turned to poison. Giving Iolas his other weapons to

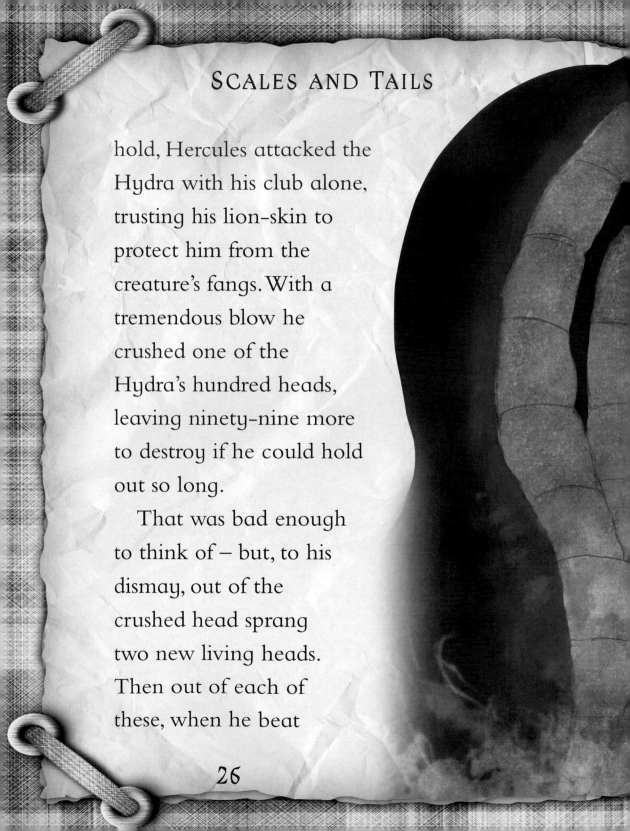

hold, Hercules attacked the Hydra with his club alone, trusting his lion-skin to protect him from the creature's fangs. With a tremendous blow he crushed one of the Hydra's hundred heads, leaving ninety-nine more to destroy if he could hold out so long.

That was bad enough to think of – but, to his dismay, out of the crushed head sprang two new living heads. Then out of each of these, when he beat

them to pieces, sprang two more, and so it was with every head the Hydra had. In truth, the more Hercules destroyed it, the stronger it grew – its hundred heads were rapidly becoming a thousand, and the thousand would become ten thousand, and so on, forever.

Just as Hercules realized the hopelessness of the labour, and was finding it work enough to ward off the innumerable fangs, a wretched crab crawled out of the ooze and seized him by the foot. He almost fainted with the sudden pain. It was too cruel, in the middle of such a battle as that, to feel

28

himself suffer this extra pain.

However, he crushed the crab under his heel, and, stopping killing the heads, contented himself with defence, while he thought what could possibly be done.

'Those first hundred heads must all have come from one head,' thought he. 'They could not grow like that without a root. So if I could only destroy the root they would stop growing. This is my mistake – I am fighting only with what I see, instead of going to the root of things and attacking the evil there.'

So he called out to Iolas to heat a piece of iron red-hot and stand by when this was ready, and to scorch with it the place of every head that the club shattered. The plan worked wonderfully. Hercules crushed head after head, Iolas burned the stumps with the red-hot iron, and so root after root was burnt up and perished. At last they came to the root of all the heads, and when this was reached and burned, the monster sputtered and died, just when Hercules felt that, strong as he was, he could scarcely strike another blow.

Hercules cut open the Hydra and dipped his arrows in its poison, so that they should give deadly wounds. Then, wearily, he returned to Mycenae hoping for a little rest.

Philip the Dragon-Slayer

E Nesbit

From a chapter of *The Magic City*

Philip has found himself shrunken and trapped with his step-sister, Lucy, inside a city he has built out of his bricks and toys. The other toys have asked him to kill a dragon.

Philip was left alone. His first act was to go up to the top of the tower and look out to see if he could see the dragon. He looked east and north and south and west. Something was moving. Something long and jointed and green. It could be nothing but the dragon.

"Oh, crikey!" said Philip, "Whatever shall I do? Perhaps I'd better see what weapons there are."

So he ran down the stairs till he came to the vaults of the castle, and there he found everything a dragon-slayer could possibly need, even a little red book called *The Young Dragon-Catcher's Guide*.

The top of the tower seemed the safest place. It was there that he tried to read the book. The words were very long and most difficultly spelt. But he did manage to make out that all dragons sleep for one hour after sunset. Then he heard a loud rattling sound from the ruin, and he knew it was the dragon who was making that sound.

As he looked, he started, and then he said

in amazement, "That old thing!"

Then he looked again, and this is what he saw. An enormous green dragon, very long and fierce-looking, that rattled as it moved, rubbing itself against the fallen pillars. And the reason Philip laughed was that he knew that dragon very well indeed. It was the clockwork lizard that had been given to him the Christmas before last.

Philip remembered that he had put it into one of the cities he had built. Only now, of course, it had grown big and had come alive like all the other live things he had put in his cities. But he saw that it was still a clockwork creature – its key was sticking out of its side. It was rubbing itself against the pillars so as to turn the key and wind itself up, but this was not half done when the sun set. The dragon instantly lay down and went to sleep.

"Well," said the Dragon-Slayer, "now I've got to think."

He did think, harder than he had ever done before. And when he had finished thinking he went down into the vault and got a long rope. Then he stood still a moment, wondering if he really were brave enough. He went out in the dusk towards the dragon.

He knew it would sleep for an hour. There it lay – about ten or twelve yards of solid dark dragon-flesh. Its metal claws gleamed in the last of the daylight. Its great mouth was open and its breathing, as it slept, was like the sound of the sea on a rough night.

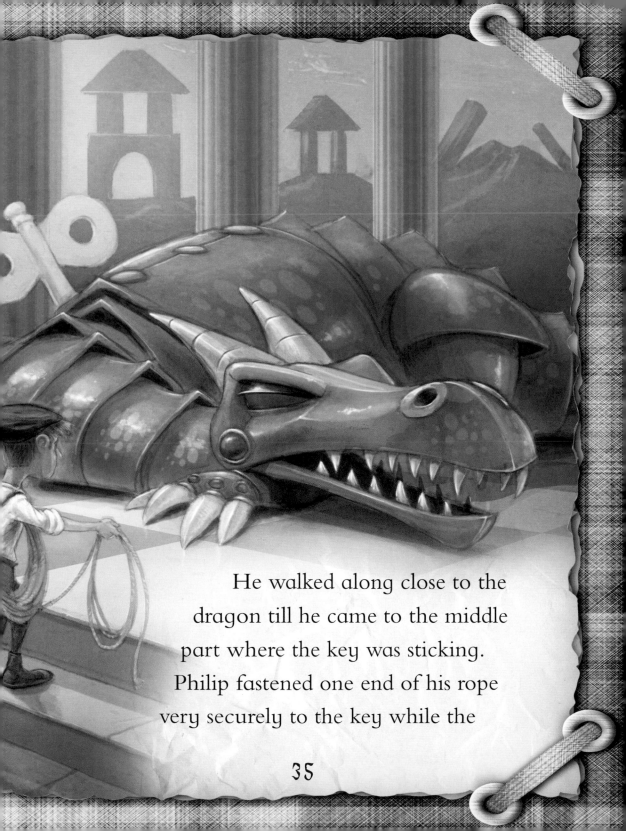

He walked along close to the
dragon till he came to the middle
part where the key was sticking.
Philip fastened one end of his rope
very securely to the key while the

dragon lay quite still. Then the Dragon-Slayer fastened the other end of the rope to the main wall of the ruin, which was very strong and firm.

You see the idea? It was really rather a clever one. When the dragon woke it would find that it was held prisoner by the rope. It would be furious and try to get free. And in its struggles it would be certain to get free, but this it could only do by detaching itself from its key. Once the key was out, the dragon would be unable to wind itself up any more and would be as good as dead. It was, as you see, an excellent plan, as far as it went.

Then the dragon woke up. Philip could see the great creature stretching itself and shaking its vast head as a dog does when it comes out of the water.

And now the dragon saw the Princess who had been placed at a convenient spot about half-way between the ruins and Philip's tower.

It threw up its snout and uttered a devastating howl, and Philip felt with a thrill of horror that, clockwork or no clockwork, the brute was alive and desperately dangerous.

It had perceived that it was bound. With great heavings and throes, with snortings and bellowings, with scratchings and tearings of its great claws and lashings of its terrible tail, it fought to be free.

Then what Philip had known would happen, did happen. With an echoing grinding rusty sound, the key was drawn from the keyhole and left still fast to its rope like an anchor to a cable.

Then something happened that Philip had not foreseen. He had forgotten that, before it fell asleep, the dragon had partly wound itself up. Its struggles had not used up all the winding. With a yell of fury it set off across the plain, wriggling its green rattling length towards the Princess!

Now there was no time to think whether one was afraid or not. Philip went down those tower stairs more quickly than he had ever gone down stairs in his life.

He put his sword over his shoulder and ran. Like

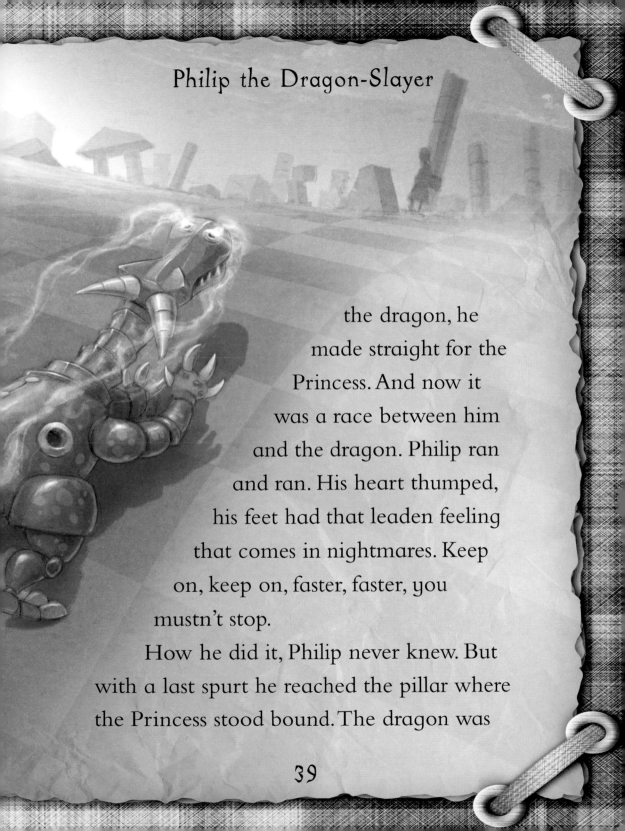

the dragon, he
made straight for the
Princess. And now it
was a race between him
and the dragon. Philip ran
and ran. His heart thumped,
his feet had that leaden feeling
that comes in nightmares. Keep
on, keep on, faster, faster, you
mustn't stop.

How he did it, Philip never knew. But
with a last spurt he reached the pillar where
the Princess stood bound. The dragon was

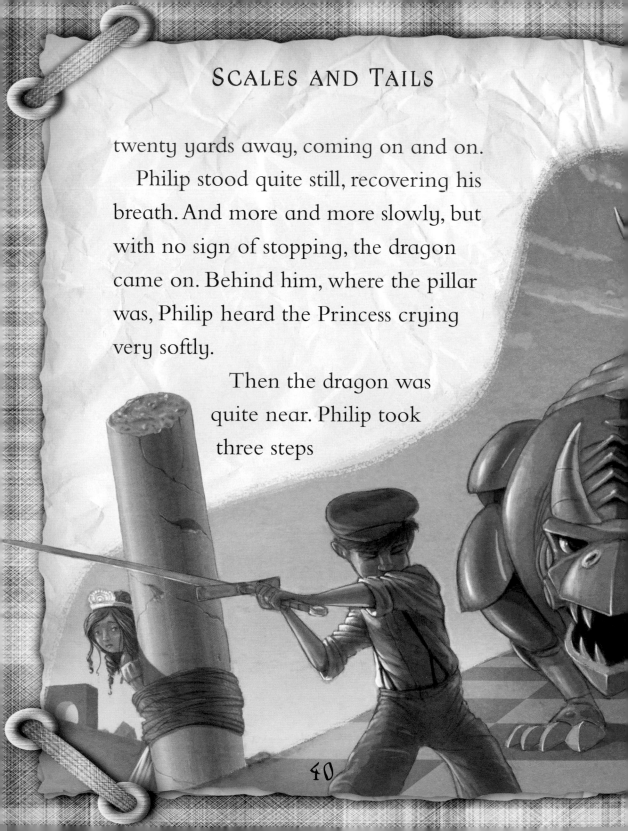

twenty yards away, coming on and on.

Philip stood quite still, recovering his breath. And more and more slowly, but with no sign of stopping, the dragon came on. Behind him, where the pillar was, Philip heard the Princess crying very softly.

Then the dragon was quite near. Philip took three steps

forward, took aim with his sword, shut his eyes and hit as hard as he could. Then something hard and heavy knocked him over, and for a time he knew no more.

When he came to himself again, Mr Noah was patting him on the back, all the people were shouting like mad, and beside him lay the dragon, lifeless and still.

"Oh!" said Philip, "did I really do it?"

"You did indeed," said Mr Noah, "however you may succeed with the other deeds, you are definitely the hero of this one. And now, if you feel well enough, prepare to receive the reward."

"Oh!" said Philip, brightening, "I didn't know there was to be a reward."

"Only the usual one," said Mr Noah. "The Princess, you know."

Philip became aware that a figure in a white veil was standing quite near him, and round its feet lay lengths of cut rope.

"The Princess is yours," said Mr Noah.

"But I don't want her," said Philip, adding by an afterthought, "thank you."

"That's not my affair," said Mr Noah. "She is waiting for you to take her by the hand and raise her veil."

"Must I?" said Philip miserably. "Well, here goes."

He took a small cold hand in one of his and with the other lifted, very gingerly, a corner of the veil. The other hand of the

Philip the Dragon-Slayer

Princess drew back the veil, and the Dragon-Slayer and the Princess were face to face.

"Why!" cried Philip "it's Lucy!"

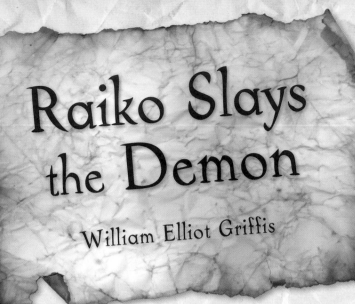

Raiko Slays the Demon

William Elliot Griffis

In the hill country of Japan grew up a brave young warrior and clever archer. On account of his skill in the use of the bow, he was called to guard the Emperor's palace. At that time, the Emperor could not sleep at night because his rest was disturbed by a frightful beast, which scared away even the soldiers in armour who stood on guard.

Raiko Slays the Demon

This dreadful beast had the wings of a bird, the body and claws of a tiger, the head of a monkey, a serpent's tail, and the crackling scales of a dragon. Every night it landed upon the roof of the palace, and howled and scratched so dreadfully that the poor Emperor grew weak and thin. None of the guards dared to face it in hand-to-hand combat, and none had skill enough to hit it with an arrow in the dark, though several of them tried.

The young archer decided to fight the beast come what might. So he strung his bow carefully, sharpened his steel-headed arrows, stored his quiver, and stood guard alone, except for his favourite servant.

It chanced to be a stormy night. The lightning was very bright, and the thunder-demon was beating all his drums. The wind swirled around frightfully, as though the wind-imp were emptying all his bags. Towards midnight, the hawk-eye of the archer saw, during a flash of lightning, the awful beast sitting at the tip of the ridge-pole, on the north-east end of the roof. He told his servant to have a torch of straw and twigs ready to light at a moment's notice. Then he fitted the notch of his best arrow into the silk cord of his bow.

Keeping his eyes strained, he soon saw the glare of one eye, now two eyes. The beast, with a swaying head, crept along the great roof to the place on the eaves directly over the Emperor's sleeping room, and there it stopped.

This was the archer's opportunity. Aiming about a foot to the right of where he saw the eye glare, he drew his yard-length arrow shaft clear back to his shoulder, and let fly. A dull thud, a frightful howl, a heavy

bump on the ground, and the writhing of some creature among the pebbles told in a few seconds' time that the arrow had struck flesh. The next instant the servant rushed out with the blazing torch and joined in the battle with his knife. A short but fierce three-cornered fight ensued, but the warrior's sharp sword soon finished the monster by cutting his throat. Then they skinned it, and the next morning the hide was shown to His Majesty.

All congratulated the brave archer on his valour and marksmanship. Many young men, sons of nobles and warriors, begged to become his pupils in archery. The Emperor ordered a noble to present him with a famous sword named 'The King of Wild

Boars' and a lovely maid of honour begged to be his wife. He was promoted to captain of the guard, and given a high-sounding title. But he was also called Raiko, and by this name he is best known to all the boys and girls in Great Japan, who tell many tales of his skill and bravery.

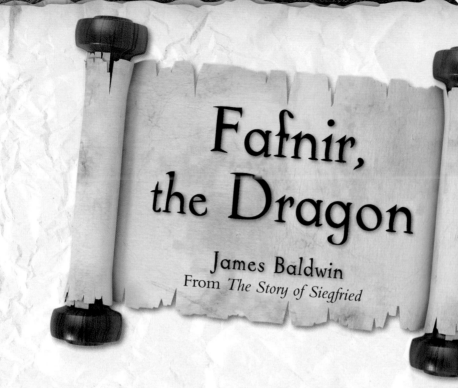

Fafnir, the Dragon

James Baldwin
From *The Story of Siegfried*

*Siegfried is a great warrior. He always travels with
Greyfell, a white horse with a gleaming mane. Siegfried
and Regin are on their way to try and kill Fafnir.*

Early in the morning, Siegfried
mounted Greyfell, and rode out
towards the desert land that lay beyond the
forest and the barren mountain range. For
seven days they wended their way through
the thick forest, sleeping at night on the

bare ground beneath the trees, while the wolves and other wild beasts of the forest filled the air with their hideous howlings. But no evil creature dared come near them, for fear of the shining beams of light which fell from Greyfell's gleaming mane.

On the eighth day they came to the open country and to the hills, where the land was covered with black boulders. No living thing was seen there, not even an insect nor a blade of grass, and the silence of the grave was over all. The earth was dry and the sun hung above them like a painted shield in a blue-black sky, and there was neither shade nor water anywhere. But Siegfried rode onwards. Towards the evening of the next day they came to a dark mountain wall that stretched far out on either side, and rose high above them.

Slowly and painfully, they climbed the steep cliff, sometimes following a narrow path that wound along the edge of a precipice, sometimes leaping from rock to rock or over some deep gorge, and sometimes picking their way among the crags and cliffs. The sun at last went down, and one by one the stars came out. The moon was rising, round and red, when Siegfried stood by Regin's side and gazed from the mountain-top down upon the Glittering Heath that lay beyond.

And a strange, weird scene it was that met his eyes. At the foot of the mountain was a river, white and cold and still. Beyond it was a smooth and barren plain, lying silent and lonely in the pale moonlight. As

Fafnir, the Dragon

Siegfried gazed upon the scene, he saw the dim outline of some hideous monster moving, and seeming all the more terrible in the uncertain light.

"It is he!" whispered Regin in fear, "It is Fafnir, the Dragon! Should we not go back? Or will you dare to go forward and meet the dragon?"

"None but cowards give up," answered Siegfried. "Go back if you are afraid, but you must go alone. You have brought me to meet the dragon of the heath. Before the setting of another sun, the deed which you have urged me to do will be done."

Then he dashed down the eastern slope of the mountain, leaving Greyfell and the trembling Regin behind him. Soon he stood on the banks of the white river, which lay between the mountain and the heath, but the stream was deep and the channel was very wide. He paused a moment, wondering how he should cross. While he stood, a boat came silently out of the mists and drew near. The boatman stood up and called to him, "What man are you who dares come into this land of loneliness and fear?"

"I am Siegfried," answered the lad, "and I have come to slay Fafnir, the Dragon."

"Sit in my boat," said the boatman, "and I will carry you across the river."

Siegfried stepped in and sat by the boatman's side, and the little vessel turned and moved towards the farther shore.

"In what way will you fight the dragon?" asked the boatman.

Fafnir, the Dragon

"With my trusty sword Balmung," answered Siegfried.

"But he breathes deathly poisons, and his eyes dart forth lightning, and no man can withstand his strength," said the boatman.

"I will find some way by which to overcome him."

"Then be wise, and listen to me," said the boatman. "As you go up from the river you will find a road, worn deep and smooth, starting from the water's edge and winding over the moor. It is the trail of Fafnir, down which he comes at dawn of every day to drink at the river. Dig a pit in this road and hide yourself within it. In the morning, when Fafnir passes over it, let him feel the edge of Balmung."

As the man ceased speaking, the boat

touched the shore, and Siegfried leapt out. He looked back to thank his unknown friend, but neither boat nor boatman was to be seen. Then the lad remembered that the strange boatman had worn a blue hood with golden stars, and that his one eye glistened and sparkled with a light that was more than human. Siegfried knew that he had talked with Odin.

Then, with a braver heart than before, he went forward along the river bank, until he came to Fafnir's trail – a deep, wide furrow in the earth, beginning at the river's bank and winding far away over the heath. The bottom of the trail was soft and slimy, and its sides had been worn smooth by Fafnir's travel through it.

In this road, Siegfried, with his trusty

sword Balmung, scooped out a deep and narrow pit. When the grey dawn began to appear in the east, he hid himself within this pit and waited for the coming of Fafnir.

He had not long to wait, for no sooner had the sky begun to redden in the light of the coming sun than the dragon was heard. Siegfried peeped from his hiding place, and saw him coming far down the road. With bloodshot eyes, gaping mouth and flaming nostrils, the hideous creature came rushing onwards. His sharp, curved claws dug deep into the soft earth, and his bat-like wings half trailed on the ground, half flapped in the air.

It was a terrible moment for Siegfried, but still he was not afraid. He crouched low down in his hiding place, and the bare blade of the trusty Balmung glittered in the morning light.

On came the hastening feet, and the red gleam from the monster's flaming nostrils lit up the pit where Siegfried lay. Then a black, inky mass rolled above him. Now was his chance. The bright edge of Balmung struck the heart of Fafnir as he passed.

The monster stopped short, while but half of his long body had glided over the pit, for sudden death had overtaken him. His horrid head fell lifeless upon the ground. His cold wings flapped once, and then lay, quivering and helpless, spread out on either side. Streams of thick, black blood flowed from his heart, through the wound beneath, and filled the trench in which Siegfried was hidden. It ran like a mountain torrent down

the road towards the river. Siegfried was covered from head to foot with the slimy liquid, and, had he not quickly leapt from his hiding place, he would have been drowned in the swift-rushing stream.

The bright sun rose in the east, covering the mountain tops, and fell upon the still waters of the river, lighting up the treeless plains around. The sound of singing birds and rippling waters – such as had not broken the silence of the Glittering Heath for ages – came to Siegfried's ears. The dragon was dead, and Nature had awakened from her sleep of dread. The shining Greyfell stood by his side.

Siegfried turned his back on the fearful scene, and rode away. So swiftly did Greyfell carry him over the desert land and

Fafnir, the Dragon

the mountain waste, that, when night came, they stood on the shore of the great North Sea and the white waves broke at their feet.

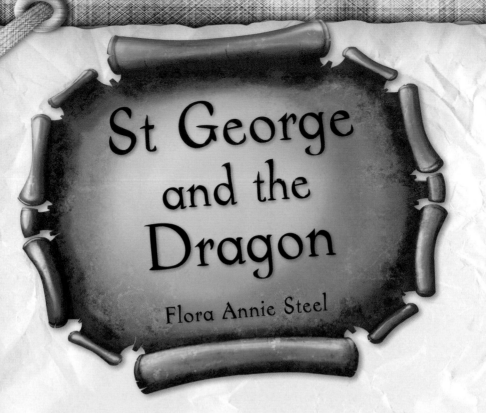

St George and the Dragon

Flora Annie Steel

St George, the bold knight, rode on his horse, Bayard, seeking to do good and fight evil. This is the story of an adventure he had in the land of Egypt.

It began when, on his travels, St George came to a chapel, where he begged to stay for the night. The monk who lived there said, "Sir Knight of Merrie England – for I see England's cross on your shield – you have come here in an evil time. We have a terrible dragon that rages up and down the country by day and by night. If he is not given an innocent maiden to devour each day, he sends a deadly plague among the people. This has not stopped for twenty and four years, so that there is only one maiden left – the beautiful Sâbia, daughter to the King. Tomorrow she will die, unless some brave knight will slay the monster. To anyone who can perform this deed, the King offers his crown and the hand of his daughter in marriage."

"I don't care about crowns," said St George boldly, "but the beautiful maiden shall not die. I will slay the monster."

So, rising at dawn of day, he buckled on his armour, laced his helmet, and with his

sword Ascalon in his
hand, he mounted
Bayard and rode into the
Valley of the Dragon.
Now on the way he met a
procession of old women weeping
and wailing, and in the middle was
the most beautiful woman he had ever
seen. St George got off his horse and bowed
low before the lady, telling her to return to
her father's palace, since he was about to
kill the dreaded dragon. The beautiful Sâbia
thanked him with smiles and tears, and he
rode on to his adventure.

Now, no sooner did the dragon catch
sight of the brave Knight than its leathery
throat sent out a sound more terrible than
thunder, and coming out from its hideous

St George and the Dragon

den, it spread its burning wings and prepared to attack. Its size and appearance might well have made the bravest man tremble. It was a full forty feet from shoulder to tail, its body was covered with green scales, its belly was as gold, and through its flaming wings the blood ran thick and red.

Its attack was so fierce, the Knight was nearly knocked to the ground. But recovering himself, St George gave the dragon a thrust with his spear. The furious monster then struck him so violently with its tail that both horse and rider were thrown over.

Now, by great good chance,
St George was flung under the
shade of a flowering orange
tree, whose scent has such
power that no poisonous
beast dare come within its
branches. So lying under the tree
he had time to recover.

When he had got his strength
back, he rose and struck the
burning dragon on his belly
with his trusty sword Ascalon. There spouted
out poison of such strength that it ate away
the armour of the bold Knight, which
dropped off him.

It might have gone very badly with
St George of Merrie England if it wasn't for
the orange tree, which once again gave him

shelter under its branches.
Then, with a bold heart, he
came forward again, and
struck the fiery dragon
under one of its flaming
wings so that the weapon
pierced its heart. All the
grass around turned crimson
with the blood that flowed
from the dying monster.

So St George of England
cut off the dreadful head and, hanging it on
a shaft of his spear that had broken, he
mounted his steed Bayard, and rode on to
the palace of the King.

Now the King's name was Ptolemy, and
when he saw that the dreaded dragon was
indeed killed, he gave orders for the city to

be decorated. He sent a golden chariot with wheels of ebony and cushions of silk to bring St George to the palace. The King also commanded a hundred noblemen dressed in crimson velvet and mounted on milk-white horses to escort him there, while musicians walked in front of him, filling the air with sweetest sounds.

The beautiful Sâbia herself washed and bandaged the weary Knight's wounds. Then, after he had been magnificently feasted, he lay down to rest, while the beautiful Sâbia from her balcony lulled him to sleep with her golden lute.

The Laidly Worm

Flora Annie Steel

'Laidly Worm' is what people in the north of England used to say to mean a hideous serpent.

In Bamborough Castle there once lived a king who had two children, a son named Childe Wynde and a daughter who was called May Margret. Their mother was dead, and the King mourned her long and faithfully. But after his son Childe Wynde went to seek his fortune, the King, hunting in the forest, came across a lady of such great beauty that he fell in love with her at once and determined to marry her.

Now Princess May Margret said nothing, though she stood long on the castle walls looking out across the sea wishing for her dear brother's return, for, you see, they had mothered each other.

Still no news came of Childe Wynde, so on the day when the old King was to bring the new Queen home, May Margret stood at the Castle gate ready to hand over the keys to her step-mother.

As the bridal procession approached with all the lords in attendance, she looked so fair and so sweet, that the lords whispered to one another of her beauty saying she was the fairest lady in all the land. The new

The Laidly Worm

Queen overheard this and she stamped her foot, and her face flushed with anger.

That same night the new Queen, who was also a witch, left her royal bed and, returning to the lonely cave where she did her magic, cast Princess May Margret under a spell with charms three times three, and passes nine times nine. And this was her spell:

"I turn you to a Laidly Worm,
  And such shall ye ever be
  Until Childe Wynde, the King's dear son,
  Comes home across the sea.

  Until the world comes to an end
  Unspelled you'll never be,
  Unless Childe Wynde of his own free will
  Shall give you kisses three!"

SCALES AND TAILS

So it came to pass that Princess May Margret went to her bed a maiden, full of grace, and rose next morning a Laidly Worm. When her maids came to dress her they found coiled up in her bed an awesome dragon, which uncoiled itself and came toward them. When they ran away terrified, the Laidly Worm crawled and

crept, and crept and crawled down to the sea. And there it curled itself round a stone and lay basking in the sun.

Then for seven miles east and seven miles west and seven miles north and south, the whole countryside knew the hunger of the Laidly Worm. It drove the awesome beast to leave its resting place at night and devour everything it came across.

At last a wise warlock told the people that if they wished to be rid of these horrors, they must take the milk of seven white cows every morning and every evening for the Laidly Worm to drink. This they did, and after that the Laidly Worm troubled the countryside no longer, but lay looking out to sea with its terrible snout in the air.

But the word of its doings had gone east and had gone west. It had even gone over the sea and had come to Childe Wynde's ears. So he called his men-at-arms together and said, "We must sail to Bamborough and kill this Laidly Worm."

Then they built a ship without delay, laying the keel with wood from the rowan tree. They made masts of rowan wood also, and set forth.

One morning the wicked Queen, looking from the castle, saw the gallant ship in Bamborough Bay, and she sent out all her witch-wives and her imps to raise a storm and sink the ship. But they came back unable to hurt it, for it was built of rowan wood, and witches have no power over that.

Then the Witch Queen laid spells upon

the Laidly Worm to attack the ship.

Now the Laidly Worm had no choice but to obey. So three times three did Childe Wynde attempt to land, and three times three the Laidly Worm kept the good ship from the shore, but he was not to be beaten. Childe Wynde rounded the next point to Budley sands, and there, jumping into the water, he got safely to land, and drawing his sword, rushed up to fight the awesome Worm. But as he raised his sword to strike he heard a voice, soft as the western wind, telling him to put up his sword and give three kisses to the Worm.

The voice seemed to him like the voice of his dear sister, May Margret. So Childe Wynde, remembering how he had loved his sister, put his arms round the Laidly Worm and kissed it once. And he kissed the loathly thing twice. And he kissed it yet a third time as he stood with the wet sand at his feet.

Then with a hiss and a roar, the Laidly Worm sank to the sand, and in his arms was May Margret!

He wrapped her in his cloak, for she trembled in the cold sea air, and carried her to Bamborough Castle. The wicked Queen, knowing her hour was come, stood, deserted

The Laidly Worm

by her imps and witch-wives, on the stairs, twisting her hands.

Then Childe Wynde, looking at her, cried, "Woe to you, wicked Queen! The curse you put on my sister shall come now upon you."

And as he spoke the wicked Queen began to shrivel, and she shrivelled and shrivelled to a wrinkled toad that hopped down the castle steps and disappeared.

To this day a loathsome toad is sometimes seen haunting Bamborough Castle, and that Laidly Toad is the wicked Witch Queen! But Childe Wynde and Princess May Margret both lived happily ever after.

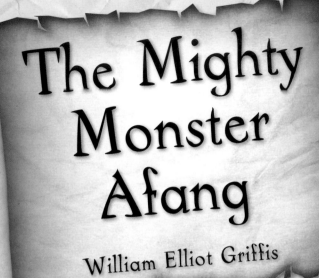

The Mighty Monster Afang

William Elliot Griffis

This story uses the old belief that a young girl could tame a monster by singing to it.

After the Welsh had come up from Cornwall into their new land, they began to cut down the trees to build towns, and to have fields and gardens.

While they were draining the swamps and bogs, they drove out the monsters that had made their lairs in these wet places.

The Mighty Monster Afang

These terrible creatures liked to poison people with their bad breath, and even ate up little boys and girls when they strayed away from home.

Now there was a great monster named the Afang that lived in a big bog, hidden among the high hills and inside of a dark, rough forest.

This ugly creature had an iron-clad back, and a long tail that could wrap itself around a mountain. It had four front legs, with big knees that were bent up like a grasshopper's, but were covered with scales like armour. These were as hard as steel, and bulged out at the thighs. Along its back, was a ridge of horns like spines, and higher than an alligator's. Against such a tough hide, when the hunters shot their darts and hurled their javelins, these weapons fell down to the ground like harmless pins.

On this great monster's head were big ears, halfway between those of a donkey and an elephant. Its eyes were round and as green as leeks, while they were as big as pumpkins.

But after its dinner, when the creature had swallowed down a man, or two calves, or four sheep, or a cow, or three goats, its body swelled up like a big balloon. Then it usually lay along the ground or in the soft mud, and felt very stupid and sleepy

The Mighty Monster Afang

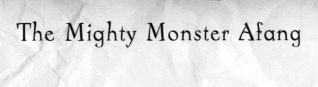

for a long while.

All around its lair lay loads of bones of creatures, girls, women, men, boys, cows, and occasionally a donkey. Someone may ask, why did not some brave man shoot the monster with a poisoned arrow, or drive a spear into him under the arms where the flesh was tender, or cut off his head with a sharp sword?

The trouble was just here. There were plenty of brave fellows ready to fight the monster, but nothing made of iron could pierce that hide of his. It was like armour.

Nothing would do, but to go up into his lair and drag him out.

But what man or company of men was strong enough to do this, when a dozen giants in a gang, with thick ropes, could hardly tackle the job?

However, one brave girl volunteered to bind the monster in his lair. She said, "I'm not afraid." Her sweetheart was named Gadern, and he was a young and strong hunter. He talked over the matter with her and they planned it together.

Gadern went all over the country, summoning the farmers to bring their ox teams and log chains. Then he set the blacksmiths to work, forging new and especially heavy chains, made of the best native iron from the mines, for which

The Mighty Monster Afang

Wales is still famous.

Meanwhile, the lovely maiden dressed herself in her prettiest clothes, arranged her hair in the most enticing way, and hung a white blossom on each side, over her ears, with one flower also at her neck.

When she had perfumed her garments, she went up the lake where the big bog and the waters were and where the monster hid himself.

While the maiden was still quite a distance away, the terrible Afang, scenting his visitor from afar, came rushing out of his lair. When very near, he reared his head high in the air, expecting to pounce on her with his iron-clad claws.

The girl was not at all afraid, but smoothed the monster's back and tickled its

neck until the Afang's throat actually qurgled with a laugh. When he did this, the people down in the valley thought it was thunder, though the sky was clear and blue.

The maiden tickled his chin, and soon she had gently lulled him to sleep, by singing a cradle song. This she did so softly

and sweetly, that in a few minutes, with its head in her lap, the monster was sound asleep and even began to snore.

Then, quietly, from their hiding places in the bushes, Gadern and his men crawled out. When near the dreaded Afang, they stood up and sneaked forward very softly on tiptoe. They had wrapped the links of the chain in grass and leaves, so that no clanking was heard. Slowly but surely they passed the chain over its body in the middle, besides tying it tightly between its fore and hind legs.

All this time, the monster slept on, for the girl kept on crooning her melody.

When the forty oxen were all harnessed together, the drivers cracked all their whips at the same time, so that it sounded like a clap of thunder, and the whole team began to pull together.

The sudden jerk made the monster angry, and its bellowing was terrible. It rolled round and round, and dug its four sets of toes, each with three claws, into the ground. It tried hard to crawl into its lair or slip into the lake.

Finding that neither was possible, the Afang looked about for some big tree to wrap its tail around. But all his writhings and plungings were of no use.

In a great hole in the ground big enough to be a pond, they dumped the Afang, and soon a little lake was formed. This strange bit of water is called 'The Lake of the Green Well'. It is considered dangerous for man or beast to go too near it. Birds do not like to fly over the surface, and when sheep tumble in, they sink to the bottom at once.

As for Gadern and his brave and lovely sweetheart, they were married and lived long and happily. All farmers honour his memory and bless the name of the lovely girl that sang the monster to sleep.

The Quarrelsome Dragons

L Frank Baum

From *The Tin Man of Oz*

Woot, a Green Monkey, and his friends have stolen a magic apron that can make anything open when you say the word 'Open'. The earth has opened underneath Woot.

The Green Monkey sank gently into the earth for a little way and then tumbled swiftly through space, landing on a rocky floor with a thump that astonished him. Then he sat up, found that no bones were broken, and gazed around him.

The Quarrelsome Dragons

He seemed to be in a big underground cave, which was dimly lit by dozens of big round discs that looked like moons. They were not moons, however, as Woot discovered when he had examined the place more carefully. They were eyes. The eyes were in the heads of enormous beasts whose bodies trailed far behind them.

Each beast was bigger than an elephant, and three times as long, and there were a dozen or more of the creatures scattered here and there about the cavern. On their bodies were big scales, as round as pie-plates, which were beautifully tinted in shades of green, purple and orange. On the ends of their long tails were clusters of bright jewels.

Woot saw that the creatures had wide

mouths and rows of terrible teeth. From tales he had heard of such beings, he knew they were the great Dragons that had been driven from the surface of the earth, and were only allowed to come out once in a hundred years to search for food.

The Green Monkey sat upon the floor where he had fallen, staring around, and the owners of the big eyes returned his look,

92

silently. Finally one of the Dragons asked, in a deep, grave voice, "What was that?"

And the greatest Dragon of all, who was just in front of the Green Monkey, answered in a still deeper voice, "It is some foolish animal from Outside."

"Is it good to eat?" inquired a smaller Dragon beside the great one. "I'm hungry."

"Hungry!" exclaimed all the Dragons together, and then the great one said, "Tut-tut, my son! You've no reason to be hungry at this time."

"Why not?" asked the little Dragon. "I haven't eaten anything in eleven years."

"Eleven years is absolutely nothing," remarked another of the Dragons, sleepily opening and closing his eyes, "I haven't feasted for eighty-seven years. Children who eat between meals should be broken of the habit."

"All I had, eleven years ago, was a rhinoceros, and that's not a full meal at all," grumbled the young one. "And before that I had waited sixty-two years to be fed, so it's no wonder I'm hungry."

"How old are you now?" asked Woot, forgetting his own danger in his interest in the conversation.

"Why, I'm – I'm – How old am I, Father?" asked the little Dragon.

"Goodness gracious! What a child to ask questions. Don't you know that thinking is very bad for Dragons?" said the big Dragon, impatiently.

"How old am I, Father?" persisted the small Dragon.

"About six hundred and thirty, I believe. Ask your mother."

"No, don't!" said an old Dragon in the background. "Haven't I enough worries, what with being wakened in the middle of a nap, without having to keep track of my children's ages?"

"You've been fast asleep for over sixty years, Mother," said the child Dragon. "How long a nap do you want?"

"I should have slept forty years longer. And this strange little green beast should be punished for falling into our cavern and disturbing us."

"I didn't know you were here, and I didn't know I was going to fall in," explained Woot.

"Nevertheless, here you are," said the

great Dragon, "and you have carelessly woken our entire tribe, so it stands to reason you must be punished."

"In what way?" inquired the Green Monkey, trembling a little.

"Give me time and I'll think of a way. You're in no hurry, are you?" asked the great Dragon.

"No, indeed," cried Woot. "Take your time. I'd much rather you'd all go to sleep again, and punish me when you wake up in a hundred years or so."

"Please let me eat him!" exclaimed the littlest Dragon.

"He is too small," said the father Dragon. "To eat this one Green Monkey would only make you hungry for more, and there are no more."

"Stop this chatter and let me get to sleep," said another Dragon, yawning in a fearful manner, for when he opened his mouth a sheet of flame leapt out from it and made Woot jump back.

In his jump he bumped against the nose

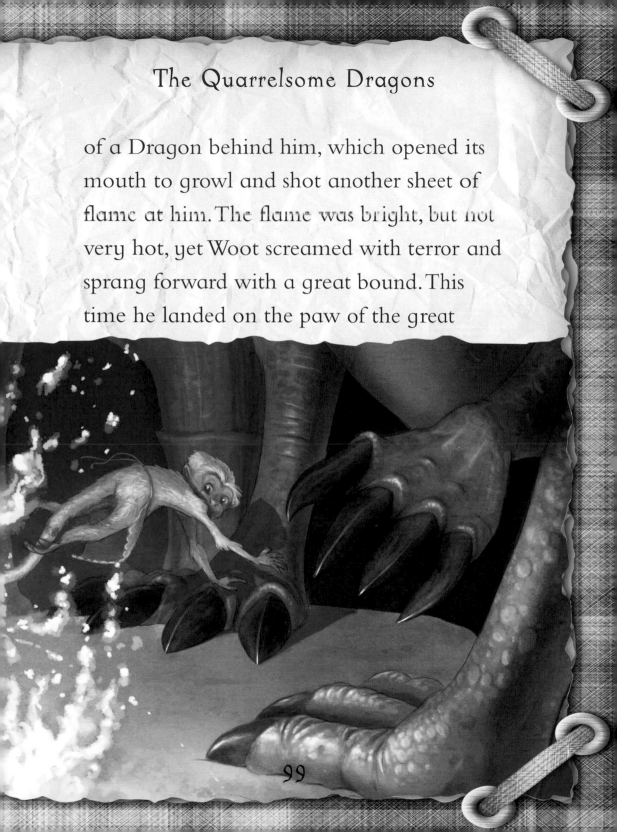

The Quarrelsome Dragons

of a Dragon behind him, which opened its mouth to growl and shot another sheet of flame at him. The flame was bright, but not very hot, yet Woot screamed with terror and sprang forward with a great bound. This time he landed on the paw of the great

Chief Dragon, who angrily raised his other front paw and struck the Green Monkey a fierce blow. Woot went sailing through the air and fell sprawling upon the rocky floor.

All the great beasts were now thoroughly awakened, and they blamed the monkey for disturbing their quiet. The littlest Dragon darted after Woot and the others followed, flashing from their eyes and mouths flames which lighted up the entire cavern. Woot almost gave up at that moment, but he scrambled to his feet and dashed away to the farthest end of the cave, the Dragons following more slowly because they were too clumsy to move fast. Perhaps they thought there was no need to hurry as the monkey could not escape from the cave.

But at the end of the place, the cavern

floor was heaped with tumbled rocks, so Woot climbed from rock to rock until he found himself crouched against the cavern roof. There he waited, for he could go no farther, while on over the tumbled rocks slowly crept the Dragons – the littlest one coming first because he was hungry as well as angry.

The beasts had almost reached him when Woot, remembering his lace apron, recovered his wits and shouted, "Open!" At the cry a hole appeared in the roof of the cavern just above his head, and through it the sunlight streamed down upon the Green Monkey.

The Dragons paused, astonished at the magic and blinking at the sunlight, and this gave Woot time to climb through the opening. As soon as he reached the surface of the earth the hole closed again, and the Green Monkey realized with a thrill of joy that he had seen the last of the dangerous Dragon family.

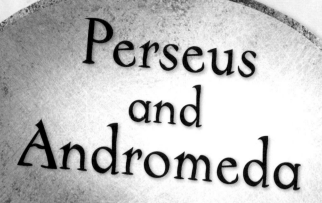

Perseus and Andromeda

R E Francillon

The great Greek hero Perseus is travelling through the lands around the Mediterranean Sea. An oracle was a priest or priestess who foretold the future and gave advice to people based on their prophecies.

Perseus continued his journey, travelling on and on until he reached the coast of Ethiopia, and entered a great city on the seashore.

But though the place seemed great and

rich, the whole air was full of sadness and gloom. The people went about silent and sighing, and had no attention to spare for a stranger. When Perseus reached the King's palace the signs of sadness were deeper still.

"What is the matter?" asked Perseus at last, seizing a passing servant by the arm. "Is it the death of the King?"

"Ah, if it were only that!" said the man. "But no, King Cepheus is alive and well. Alas, and woe is me!" And so once more he fell to wailing, and passed on.

Over and over again Perseus tried to get an answer, but heard nothing but tears and groans. And so he went on till he reached a chamber where sat the King himself in the midst of his court.

"I see you are a stranger," said King

Perseus and Andromeda

Cepheus. "Pardon us if we have seemed unfriendly and unlike the Ethiopians, the friends of the gods. It is not our way. But," he continued, the tears flowing as he spoke, "if you knew, you would understand."

"Let me know," said Perseus gently, for he was filled with pity for the King's tears.

"My daughter, Princess Andromeda," answered the King, "is condemned to a horrible death. I do not know whether she is yet alive."

"How can a king's daughter be condemned to death against her father's will?" asked Perseus.

"No wonder it sounds strange," answered Cepheus, "but listen, Andromeda is my only child. For some reason the gods have permitted our land to be attacked by a monster that comes out of the sea and that spares neither man, woman, nor child. Not one of us is left without cause to mourn. Fearing that all my people would be destroyed, I asked the great oracle of Ammon in what way the monster could be stopped. Alas! The oracle said that the only thing that would work would be delivering up Andromeda herself to be eaten. What could I do? Could I let my people lose all their children for the sake of my own? There was only one thing for a king, who is the father of all his people, to do, and even now—" But he could say no more.

"Oracle or no oracle," said Perseus, "it shall not be while I am alive! Where is the princess now?"

"She was chained at sunrise to a rock on

the seashore, there to wait for the monster. But where she is now—"

Perseus did not wait for another word, but, leaving the palace, hurried along the shore, already half covered by the rising tide. At last he came to what made his heart beat and burn with pity and rage. Chained by her wrists to a pillar of rock was the most beautiful of all princesses, already nearly waist-high in the rising waves. What struck Perseus most was her look of quiet courage and noble pride – the look of one who was devoting herself to a cruel death for the country's sake, and in order that others might be saved.

The whole heart of Perseus went out to her. He vowed, if he could not save her, to share her death. But before he could reach her side, a huge black wave parted, and out came the monster – a creature like nothing else of land or sea, with a swollen, shapeless body, studded with hungry, cruel eyes, and hundreds of long, slimy limbs, twisting and crawling, each with a yawning mouth, from which streamed fire and horrible fumes.

Andromeda turned pale as the creature came on with a slowness more dreadful than speed. Perseus could not wait. Springing from the rock he threw himself, like lightning, full upon the monster, and then began such a struggle as had never been seen before. The creature twined its limbs around Perseus, and tried to crush him. As soon as Perseus tore himself from one, he was clutched by another.

Perseus felt his life passing from him. He

put all the strength he had left into one last
blow. It fell only on the monster's right
shoulder. But that was the one place where
it could be pierced. The coils relaxed, and
Perseus, to his own amazement, saw the

monster floating, a shapeless corpse, upon the waves.

Having released Andromeda, who had watched the struggle in dread for what had seemed the certain fate of her rescuer, he carried her back to her father's palace. I need not tell how the mourning turned into wonder and joy!

"What can I do to show my gratitude?" asked King Cepheus of Perseus. "Ask of me whatever you will, and it shall be yours, on the word of a king!"

"If she is willing, give me Andromeda to be my wife," said Perseus. "That is all I want in the world."

"Gladly," said Cepheus, but suddenly he looked serious. "I have promised you on the word of a king, which cannot be broken.

But I must warn you that you are not the first in the field. Andromeda has long been claimed in marriage by the powerful Prince Phineus, and he is not the man to lose what he wants without giving trouble."

"He never gave any trouble to the monster," said Perseus, thinking that Cepheus, though kind, was rather a weak and timid sort of king. So the marriage of Perseus and Andromeda was settled to the great joy of both, and all the nobles were invited to a great festival in honour of the wedding, and of the delivery of the land.

BOGGARTS, TROLLS AND GOBLINS

Farmer Griggs's Boggart	114
How an Old Man Lost His Wart	125
The Farmer and the Boggart	137
How the Goblins Turned to Stone	142
The Christmas Goblins	152
The Goblin's Arm	164
The Troll and the Bear	174
The Nix in Mischief	180
The Widow's Son	190
The Troll Who Wrote a Letter	202

Farmer Griggs's Boggart

Howard Pyle

From *Pepper and Salt*

Did you ever hear of a boggart? No? Then I will tell you. A boggart is a small imp that lives in a man's house, unseen by anyone, doing a little good but a lot of harm. Even now you may find a boggart in some houses.

The snow lay all over the ground, like soft feathers. Icicles hung down from the roof of the farmhouse, and birds crouched shivering in the bare, leafless hedgerows.

But inside the farmhouse all was warm and pleasant. Great logs snapped and crackled and roared in the wide chimney place, and Farmer Griggs sat warming his feet at the blaze.

Dame Griggs's spinning wheel went *humm-m-m*, *hum-m-m-m-m*, the cat purred in the warmth of the fire and the dog basked in the blaze.

But, *rap! tap! tap!* came a loud knock at the door.

So Farmer Griggs took his pipe out of his mouth and went to see who was there.

"Will you let me in out of the cold, Georgie Griggs?" piped a small voice. Farmer Griggs looked down and saw a little creature no taller than his knee standing in the snow on the doorstep. His face was brown and he looked up at the farmer with great eyes as bright as those of a toad. His feet were bare and he wore no clothes.

"Who are you, little man?" said Farmer Griggs.

"I'm a boggart, at your service, Georgie Griggs."

"No, no," said Farmer Griggs, "I'll give no room in my house to the likes of you." And he went to shut the door in the face of the little monster.

"But listen, Georgie Griggs," said the boggart, "I will work well for you."

Farmer Griggs's Boggart

Then Farmer Griggs did listen. "What will you do for me, then?" he asked.

"I'll tend your fires," said the little monster, "I'll bake your bread, I'll wash your dishes, I'll clean your pans, I'll scrub your floors, I'll brew your beer, I'll roast your meat, I'll boil your water, I'll stuff your sausages, I'll skim your milk, I'll make your butter, I'll knit your stockings, I'll mend your clothes, I'll patch your shoes – I'll be everywhere and do all of the work in your house!"

"I don't know," said Farmer Griggs, scratching his head doubtfully. "It's a bad thing letting mischief into the house! You're better outside, I'm quite sure."

"Shut the door, Georgie!" called out Dame Griggs.

Then Farmer Griggs shut the door, but the boggart was on the inside.

This is the way in which the boggart came into Farmer Griggs's house, and there he was to stay, for it is no easy matter getting rid of the likes of him once he is inside, I can tell you.

The boggart went over to the warm fire straight away. The cat spat at him in anger and jumped up on the dresser. But the boggart laid himself comfortably down among the warm ashes.

Now, imps, like this boggart, can only be seen as the frost is seen – when it is cold. So as the boggart grew warmer and warmer, he grew thinner and thinner! At last, when he had become thoroughly warmed through, Farmer Griggs and the dame could see him no more. But he was in the house and he stayed there.

For a time everything went smoothly. All of the housework was done as though by magic. The boggart did all that he had promised – he was everywhere and did all of the work in the house.

But after a time, the boggart began to play his pranks. He skimmed the children's milk so that they had nothing but watery stuff to pour over their porridge. He blew out the lights so that they were all in the dark, he made the fires burn cold, and he played one hundred and forty other impish tricks of the like.

However, the boggart did his housework well, so Farmer Griggs put up with his evil ways for as long as he could. At last the time came when he could bear it no longer. He knew you could not make a boggart leave a house once it was in, so Farmer Griggs decided they must go themselves.

So one fine bright day, they packed all of their belongings into a great cart and set off to find a new home.

As they came to the bottom of Shooter's Hill, who should they meet but their good neighbour, Jerry Jinks. "So, Georgie," he said, "you're leaving the old house at last?"

"Hi, Jerry," said Georgie. "We were forced to it, neighbour, for that boggart torments us so that there was no rest."

Now on the cart was a tall, upright

Farmer Griggs's Boggart

churn. As soon as Georgie Griggs had finished talking, the lid of the churn began to *clipper-clapper*, and who should speak out of it but the boggart himself. "Ay, Jerry!" said the boggart, "We're moving, man! Come and see us soon!"

"What!" cried Georgie Griggs, "Are you

there, imp? Dang it! We'll all go back to the old house, then."

So back they went again – with boggart and all.

You see, if you warm an imp by your fire, he will soon turn the whole house topsy-turvy. One cannot get rid of a boggart by going from here to there, for it is sure to be in the cart with the household things.

But how did Georgie Griggs get rid of his boggart? I will tell you.

He went to see Father Grimes, the wise man who lived in a little house on the moor. "Father Grimes," said Farmer Griggs, "how should I get rid of my boggart?"

Then Father Grimes told him to take this and that, and to do thus and so with them, and see what followed. So Farmer

Farmer Griggs's Boggart

Griggs went and bought a pretty red coat, a neat pair of blue breeches and a nice velvet cap with a bell at the top of it. Then he went to Thomas the shoemaker's and got a fine pair of shoes. He laid them on a warm spot on the hearth where the boggart used to come to sleep at night. Then he and Dame Griggs hid and watched to see what would follow.

Presently in came the boggart, whisking here and dancing there, though neither the farmer nor the dame could see him any more than if he had been a puff of wind.

"Heigh-ho!" cried the boggart, "These are fine things for sure." He put them on and began dancing until he made the ashes on the hearth spin around. He went singing and dancing, and skipping and leaping, out of the house and away. As for Georgie Griggs and his dame, they never heard a squeak from him again.

And so it was that Farmer Griggs finally got rid of his boggart.

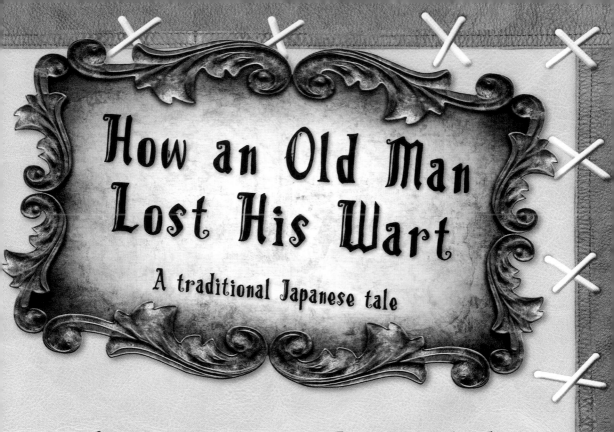

How an Old Man Lost His Wart

A traditional Japanese tale

Many many years ago in Japan there lived a good old man who had a wart like a tennis ball growing out of his right cheek. He tried everything he could think of to get rid of it, but it was all of no use.

One day the old man ran out of firewood, so he took his axe and set out for the woods up among the hills. When the day began to draw to a close he started homewards.

The old man had not gone far on his way down the mountain when the sky clouded and rain began to fall heavily. He looked about for some shelter and at last he spied the hollow trunk of a tree. He crept in easily and sat down.

At last, the sky cleared as the sun started to set. The old man was about to step out from his hiding place when he saw hundreds of goblins coming towards the spot. Some of the goblins

How an Old Man Lost His Wart

were as large as giants, others had great big eyes, others had hugely long noses, and some had such big mouths that they opened from ear to ear. All of the goblins had horns growing on their foreheads. While the old man was sitting there in terror, he heard the sounds of music and then some of the goblins began to sing.

On peeping out, the old man saw that the Goblin Chief himself was actually sitting with his back against the hollow tree, and all the other goblins were sitting round him – some drinking and some dancing. It made the old man laugh to see their strange antics.

He was so interested and excited in watching all that the goblins were doing that he forgot himself, and stepped out of the tree and stood looking on.

The Goblin Chief was taking a big cup of wine and watching one of the goblins dancing. In a little while he said with a bored air, "Isn't there any one among you all who can dance better than this?"

The old man had been fond of dancing all his life and he knew that he could do much better than the goblin.

"Shall I go and dance before these goblins and let them see what a human being can do? It might be dangerous, for if I don't please them they may kill me!" said the old fellow to himself.

However, his fears were soon overcome by his love of dancing. In a few minutes he stepped out before the whole party of goblins and began to dance at once.

"How strange!" exclaimed the horned Goblin Chief. "I've never seen such a skilful dancer before!"

When the old man had finished his dance, the big goblin said, "Thank you very much for your amusing dance. You must come often. Your skill has given us much pleasure."

The old man thanked him (while all the time planning never to come near the spot ever again).

"Will you come again tomorrow old man?" asked the goblin.

"Certainly I will," answered the old man (but not meaning it).

"What is the best thing he can leave with us as a pledge that he will keep his word?" asked the Goblin Chief, looking round.

Then one of the goblin's attendants, kneeling behind the chief, said, "The token he leaves with us must be the most important thing in his possession. I see the old man has a wart on his right cheek. I believe humans consider such a wart very lucky. Let my lord take the lump from the old man's right cheek and he will surely come tomorrow, if only to get that back."

"You are very clever," said the Goblin Chief. Then he stretched out a hairy arm and claw-like hand, and took the great lump from the old man's right cheek. Strange to say, it came off as easily as a

ripe plum from a tree, and then the merry troop of goblins suddenly vanished.

Then the old man realized how late it was and began to hurry home. He patted his right cheek all the time, as if to make sure of his good luck in having lost his wart. He was so happy that he found it impossible to walk quietly – he ran and danced the whole way home.

The old man found his wife very worried, wondering what had happened to make him so late. He soon told her all that had passed. She was as happy as her husband when he showed her that the ugly lump had disappeared from his face.

Now, next door to this good old couple there lived a wicked and disagreeable old man. He also had a wart on his left cheek and had tried all manner of things to get rid of it, but all in vain.

He heard at once of his neighbour's good luck in losing the lump on his face, so he called that very evening and asked his friend to tell him all about it. The good old man told him what had happened, and the wicked old man decided to see if he could have the same luck.

He started out the very next afternoon, and after hunting about for some time, came to the hollow tree trunk his friend had described. Here, he hid himself and waited for the twilight.

Just as he had been told, the band of goblins came at that hour and held a feast with dancing and singing. When this had gone on for some time the chief of the goblins looked around and said, "It is now time for the old man to come as he promised us. Why doesn't he come?"

When the wicked old man heard these

words he ran out of his hiding place in the tree and said, "Here I am!"

"Ah, you are the old man of yesterday," said the Goblin Chief, who could not tell humans apart. "Thank you for coming. You must dance for us."

The old man now stood up, opened his fan and began to dance. But he had never learned to dance and he thought that anything would please the goblins, so he just hopped about, waving his arms and stamping his feet.

The goblins said among themselves, "How badly he dances today!"

Then the Goblin Chief said to the old man, "Your performance today is quite different from the dance of yesterday. We don't wish to see any more of such dancing.

How an Old Man Lost His Wart

We will give you back the pledge you left with us. You must go away at once."

With these words he took out the wart that he had taken from the face of the old man who had danced so well the day before, and threw it at the right cheek of the old man who stood before him.

The lump immediately attached itself to his cheek as firmly as if it had grown there always, and all attempts to pull it off were useless. The wicked old man put one hand and then the other to each side of his face to make sure he was not dreaming a horrible nightmare. No, sure enough there was now a great wart on the right side of his face as well as on the left. The goblins had all disappeared and there was nothing for him to do but to return home.

The Farmer and the Boggart

Anon

The boggart lives under the ground in the north of England. He looks a little like a squat, hairy man with pointed teeth and arms as long as a rake. Now, once upon a time a man bought a piece of land. He went out to look at it, but as he was staring with pleasure at the good earth and planning what crop to plant, a boggart burst out of the earth in front of him and

told him to go away.
"Tis my land here,"
shrieked the boggart,
"my land, my
treasure, mine."

The farmer was a
bold man and not afraid of
the boggart. He suggested they went to see
what the lawyers would say about that. The
boggart didn't like the sound of that, for he
had a fear of towns and houses, and
suggested instead that they should share
anything that grew on the land equally.

"Very well," said the farmer, "will you
take what grows above the ground, or what
grows beneath the ground? Only mind that
you stick to your word, for I'll have no
chopping and changing once we're settled."

The Farmer and the Boggart

The boggart thought about oats and corn and rye and peas, and settled to take what grows above the ground. So the farmer planted potatoes. When the time came to divide up the crop, the farmer had a fine store for his winter food, while all the boggart got was bitter leaves and tough stalks and no crop at all. So he made a great fuss and said that next year he would take whatever grew below the ground.

"Very well," said the farmer, "I'm suited if you are." He sowed his land with wheat, which grew a fine crop for the farmer to make his bread out of, while the boggart got nothing but muddy roots.

The boggart was very angry. He demanded that next year wheat must be sown again, but this time whoever could

mow the most with
their scythe should
get the whole crop.

"Very well," said
the farmer, "I'm
agreed if you are."
When the time
came for the wheat
to be mown, the
farmer went to the
field with his scythe.
He started at one corner
and the boggart started at the
other, but what the boggart didn't know
was that the farmer had stuck iron rods in
among the stalks of corn. These wore down
the boggart's strength and took all the sharp
edge off his scythe. So the boggart stopped

The Farmer and the Boggart

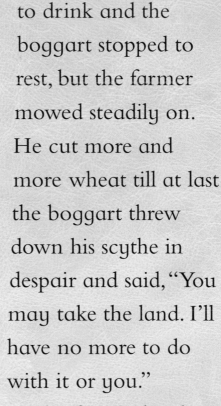

to drink and the boggart stopped to rest, but the farmer mowed steadily on. He cut more and more wheat till at last the boggart threw down his scythe in despair and said, "You may take the land. I'll have no more to do with it or you."

The farmer lived happily ever after but the boggart was never seen in that part of the country again.

How the Goblins Turned to Stone

William Elliot Griffis

The monster goblins that used to live in Holland were ugly, short fellows, very smart, quick in action and able to travel far in a second. They had big heads, green eyes and split feet, like cows. They were so ugly that they were ordered to live underground and never come out during the day. If they did, they would be turned to stone.

The ruler of the goblins lived beneath the

How the Goblins Turned to Stone

earth as the king of the underworld. His palace was made of gold and glittered with gems. All the goblins who worked in the mines and at the forges and anvils, making swords, spears, bells and jewels, obeyed him.

The most wonderful thing about these monsters was the way in which they made themselves invisible while at their mischief. This was a little red cap that every goblin possessed, and which he was careful never to lose, for while under it, no goblin could be seen by human eyes.

One night, as a dear old lady lay ill in her bed, a middle-sized goblin, with his red cap on, came through a crack into the room and stood at the foot of her bed. Just for mischief and to frighten her by making himself visible, he took off his red cap.

When the old lady saw the imp she cried out loudly, "Go away, go away." But the goblin monster only laughed at her.

Calling her daughter, Alida, the old lady whispered in her ear, "Bring me my wooden shoes straight away."

Rising up in her bed, the old lady hurled the heavy clogs, one after the other, at the goblin's head. At this, he started to get out through the crack and away, but just as he squeezed through, Alida snatched his red cap away. Twirling the little red cap around on her forefinger, a brilliant thought struck her. She went and told the men her plan, and they agreed to it. This was to gather hundreds of farmers, townfolk, boys and men together on the next moonlit night, and round up all the goblins in the town.

How the Goblins Turned to Stone

By pulling off their red caps and holding them till the sun rose, they would all be turned to stone.

Knowing that the goblin would come the next night to steal back his red cap, she left a note outside the crack telling him to bring several hundred goblins to the great moor at midnight the next day. There he would find the red cap on a bush. With his companions he could celebrate the return of the cap. In return, she asked the goblin to bring her a gold necklace.

The moonlit night came round and hundreds of the men gathered together. The plan was to move together in a circle towards the centre, where Alida was to hang the red cap upon a bush. Then, with a rush, the men were to snatch off all the goblins' caps, pulling and grabbing, whether they could see or feel anything or not.

The placing of the red cap upon the bush in the centre by Alida was the signal.

So when the great round-up narrowed to a small space, the men began to grab, snatch and pull. Putting their hands out in the air at the height of about a yard from the ground, they hustled and pushed hard. In a few minutes, hundreds of red caps were in their hands and as many goblins became visible. They were indeed an ugly collection.

But hundreds of other goblins escaped with their caps on and were still invisible. However, as they broke

How the Goblins Turned to Stone

How the Goblins Turned to Stone

away in groups they were seen, for in each bunch one or more fellow was visible because he wasn't wearing his cap. So the men divided into squads to chase the monsters. The racket kept up till the sky in the east was grey. The goblins were anxious to help their fellows or to get back their own caps, fearing the disgrace of returning bare-headed to their king and getting a good scolding. So before they even knew it was day, the sun suddenly rose on them. At the first ray of the sun, the goblins were all turned to stone.

The treeless, desolate land that, a moment before, was full of struggling goblins and men, became as quiet as the blue sky above. Nothing but some groups of rounded rocks and stones remained of the ugly goblins.

There these groups of rocks and stones, big and little, lie to this day. Among the buckwheat and the potato blossoms of the summer, under the shadows and clouds and whispering breezes of autumn, and covered with the snows of winter, they can be seen on deserted heaths.

Over some of the rocks and stones, oak trees, centuries old, have grown. Others are near or among the farmers' grain fields, or not far from houses and barnyards.

The cows wander and graze among the

How the Goblins Turned to Stone

groups of rocks and stones knowing nothing
of their past and how they got there.
  And the monster goblins come no more.

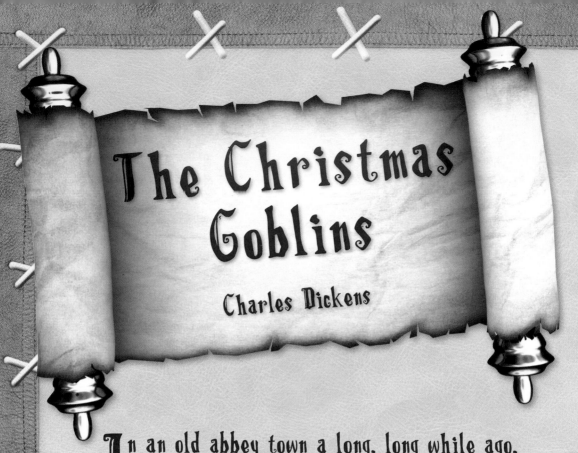

The Christmas Goblins

Charles Dickens

In an old abbey town a long, long while ago, there worked as sexton and gravedigger in the churchyard one Gabriel Grubb. He was a cross, surly fellow who mixed with nobody but himself and an old wicker bottle, which fitted into his large, deep waistcoat pocket.

A little before twilight one Christmas Eve, Gabriel put his spade on his shoulder, lit his

The Christmas Goblins

lantern and took himself towards the old churchyard. He had a grave to finish digging by the next morning and, feeling very low, he thought it might raise his spirits if he got on with his work at once.

Gabriel Grubb strode along until he turned into the dark lane that led to the churchyard. It was a gloomy, mournful place into which the townspeople did not care to go except in broad daylight, so he was very cross to hear a young boy roaring out some jolly song about having a merry Christmas.

Gabriel waited until the boy came up, then rapped him over the head with his lantern five or six times to teach him to lower his voice. As the boy hurried away with his hand to his head, Gabriel Grubb chuckled to himself and entered the churchyard, locking the gate behind him.

He took off his coat, put down his lantern and, getting into an unfinished grave, worked at digging it for an hour or so with strong determination.

But the earth was hardened with the frost, and it was no easy task to break it up and shovel it out.

At any other time this would have made Gabriel very miserable. However, he was so pleased at having stopped the small boy's singing that he took little heed of the small progress he had made when he finished work for the night.

Gabriel Grubb looked down into the grave with grim satisfaction. He murmured to himself as he gathered up his things,

The Christmas Goblins

"Brave lodgings for one, brave lodgings
    for one,
  A few feet of cold earth when life is
    done."

"Ho! ho!" he laughed, as he set himself down on a flat tombstone, which was a favourite resting place of his, and drew forth his wicker bottle. "A coffin at Christmas. A Christmas box. Ho! ho! ho!"

"Ho! ho! ho!" repeated a voice close beside him.

"It was the echoes," said he, raising the bottle to his lips again.

"It was not," said a deep voice.

Gabriel Grubb started up quickly and stood rooted to the spot with terror, for his eyes rested on a form that made his blood run cold.

The Christmas Goblins

Seated on an upright tombstone close to him was a strange, unearthly figure. It was sitting perfectly still, grinning at Gabriel Grubb with such a grin as only a goblin could call up.

"What are you doing here on Christmas Eve?" said the goblin sternly.

"I came to dig a grave, sir," stammered Gabriel Grubb.

"What man wanders among graves on such a night as this?" cried the goblin.

"Gabriel Grubb! Gabriel Grubb!" screamed a wild chorus of voices that seemed to fill the churchyard.

"What have you got in that bottle?" said the goblin.

"Gin, sir," replied Gabriel, trembling more than ever.

"Who drinks gin alone, and in a churchyard on such a night as this?"

"Gabriel Grubb! Gabriel Grubb!" exclaimed the wild voices again.

"And who, then, is our lawful prisoner?" exclaimed the goblin, raising his voice.

The invisible chorus replied, "Gabriel Grubb! Gabriel Grubb!"

"Well, Gabriel, what do you say to this?" said the goblin, as he grinned a broader grin than before.

Gabriel Grubb gasped for breath.

"What do you think of this, Gabriel?"

"It's — it's very curious, sir, very curious, sir, and very pretty," replied Gabriel, half dead with fright. "But I think I'll go back and finish my work, sir, if you please."

"Work!" said the goblin, "What work?"

The Christmas Goblins

"The grave, sir."

"Oh! The grave, eh? Who makes graves at a time when other men are merry, and takes pleasure in it?"

Again the voices replied, "Gabriel Grubb! Gabriel Grubb!"

"I'm afraid my friends want you, Gabriel," said the goblin.

"I'm sorry, sir," replied the horror-stricken Gabriel, "I don't think they can. They don't know me, sir. I don't think the gentlemen have ever seen me."

"Oh! Yes, they have. We know the man who struck the boy in the bitterness of his heart because the boy could be merry and he could not."

Here the goblin gave a loud, shrill laugh, which the echoes returned.

"I – I am afraid I must leave you, sir," said Gabriel, making an effort to move.

"Leave us!" said the goblin, "Ho! ho! ho!"

As the goblin laughed, he suddenly darted towards Gabriel, laid his hand upon his collar and sank with him through the earth. When Gabriel had had time to fetch his breath he found himself in what appeared to be a large cavern, surrounded on all sides by goblins, ugly and grim.

"And now," said the King of the Goblins, seated in the centre of the room on an elevated seat, "show the man of misery and gloom the pictures from our storehouses."

As the goblin said this a cloud rolled gradually away and showed a small, barely furnished, but neat, apartment. Little children were gathered round a bright fire,

The Christmas Goblins

clinging to their mother's gown or playing round her chair. A simple meal was spread upon the table and a chair was placed near the fire. Soon the father entered and the children ran to meet him. As he sat down to his meal the mother sat by his side and all seemed happy and comfortable.

"So what do you think of that?" the goblin asked.

Gabriel murmured something about it being very pretty.

"Show him some more," said the goblin.

Many a time the cloud went and came, and many a lesson it taught to Gabriel Grubb. He saw that men who worked hard and earned their little bit of bread were cheerful and happy. He came to the conclusion that it was a very respectable sort of world after all. No sooner had he decided this than the cloud that closed over the last picture seemed to settle on his senses and lull him to rest. One by one the goblins faded from his sight and, as the last one disappeared, he sank to sleep.

The Christmas Goblins

The day had broken when Gabriel awoke and he found himself lying on the flat gravestone, with the wicker bottle empty by his side. He got to his feet as well as he could and, brushing the frost off his coat, turned towards the town.

But Gabriel Grubb was an altered man. He had learned lessons of gentleness and good nature by his strange adventures in the goblin's cavern.

The Goblin's Arm

William Elliot Griffis

*Raiko and his brave companion, Tsuna, are great heroes in
Japanese fairy tales. Onis are terrifying goblins or demons
with horns on their heads and tusks in their mouths.*

Under Captain Raiko were three brave
guardsmen, one of whom was named
Tsuna. The duty of these men-at-arms was
to watch at the gates leading to the palace.
It had become dangerous in the city, so
many good people were afraid to go out

The Goblin's Arm

into the streets at night. Worse than all else
was the report that hill-goblins, called onis
in Japan, were prowling around in the dark.
They would seize people by the hair of their
heads, then they would drag them away to
the mountains.

The worst place in the town, to which
the two-horned goblin came most often,
was at the south-western gate. To this post
of danger, Raiko sent Tsuna, the bravest of
his guards.

It was on a dark, rainy and dismal night
that Tsuna started, well-armed, to stand
guard at the gate. Tsuna's trusty helmet was
knotted over his chin and all the pieces of
his armour were well laced up. His sandals
were tight on his feet, and in his belt was
thrust his trusty sword, freshly sharpened

until its edge was like a razor's, and with it he could cut in half a hair floating in the air.

Tsuna paced up and down the stone way with his eyes and ears wide open. The wind was blowing frightfully, the storm howled, and the rain fell in such torrents that soon the cords of Tsuna's armour and his tunic were soaked through.

The great bronze bell of the temple on the hill boomed out the hours one after another, until a single stroke told Tsuna it was the hour of midnight.

Two hours passed and still Tsuna was wide awake. The storm had calmed, but it was darker than ever. The hour of three rang out and the soft mellow notes of the temple bell died away.

The warrior, almost without knowing it,

The Goblin's Arm

grew sleepy and fell into a doze. Then he started and woke up. Tsuna shook himself, jingled his armour, pinched himself, and even pulled out his little knife and pricked his leg with the point of it to keep himself awake, but all in vain. Overcome by drowsiness, he leant against the gatepost and fell asleep.

This was just what the oni wanted. All the time it had been squatting on the cross-piece at the top of the gate waiting for his

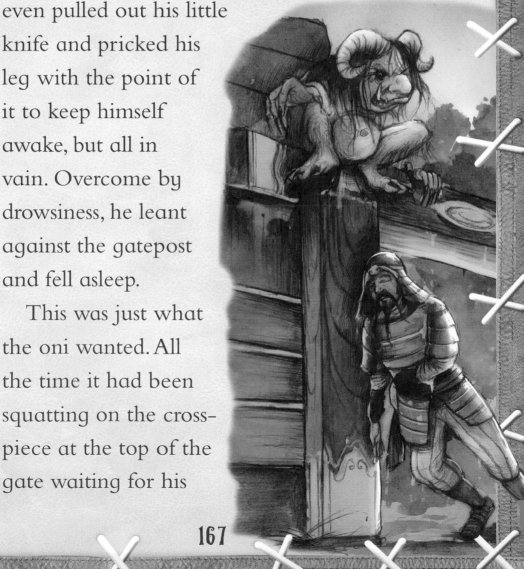

167

opportunity. Now, the oni slid down as softly as a monkey and, with its iron-like claws, grabbed Tsuna by the helmet and began to drag him into the air.

In an instant Tsuna was awake. Seizing the goblin's hairy wrist with his left hand, he drew his sword with his right, swept it round his head and cut off the oni's arm. Frightened and howling with pain, the creature

The Goblin's Arm

leapt from the post and disappeared into the clouds.

Tsuna waited with drawn sword in hand, but in a few hours it was morning. The sun rose on the pagodas and gardens and temples of the capital city. Everything was beautiful and bright. Tsuna returned to report to his captain, carrying the goblin's arm in triumph. Raiko examined it and praised Tsuna loudly for his bravery, then rewarded him with a silken sash.

Now, it is said that if a goblin's arm be cut off it can be joined with the body again if it is found within a week. So Raiko warned Tsuna to lock it up and watch it night and day, in case it is stolen from him.

Tsuna went to the stone-cutters and bought a strong box cut out of the solid stone. It had a heavy lid on it, which slid in a groove and came out only by touching a secret spring. Into this he put the arm. Then setting it in his bedchamber, he guarded it day and night, keeping the gate and all his doors locked. He didn't allow anyone who was a stranger to look at the trophy.

Six days passed by and Tsuna began to think he was safe, for all of his doors were tightly shut. So he set the box out in the middle of the room and sat down in ease before it. He took off his armour and put on his court robes. During the evening but rather late, there was a feeble knock, like that of an old woman, at the gate outside.

Tsuna cried out, "Who's there?"

The squeaky voice of his aunt, as it seemed, who was a very old woman, replied, "I want to see my nephew to praise him for his bravery in cutting the goblin's arm off."

So Tsuna let her in and carefully locked the door behind her. Tsuna helped her into the room, where she sat down on the mats in front of the box, very close to it. Then she grew talkative and praised Tsuna until he felt very proud.

All the time the old woman's left shoulder was covered with her dress, while her right hand was out. Finally she begged to be allowed to see the arm. Tsuna at first politely refused, but she urged until he slid back the stone lid just a little.

"This is my arm!" cried the old woman, turning into a goblin and dragging it out of the casket.

The goblin flew up to the ceiling and was out through the roof in a twinkling. Tsuna rushed out of the house to shoot it with an arrow, but he could just

The Goblin's Arm

see the goblin far off in the clouds, grinning horribly. As he watched, he saw the cut-off arm join again with the body, and the goblin shook *both* fists at him in victory.

The Troll and the Bear

A traditional Norwegian tale

Once upon a time, in the olden days in Norway, there was a farm in the mountains where nobody could stay over on Christmas Eve. All the folk had to go down to the old farm in the valley and spend Christmas there. For every Christmas Eve an ugly troll came lumbering down from the high peaks with a sackful of toads on his back, and he made himself

comfortable in front of the
farm's fire. There he would
sit, toasting toads
and popping
them in his
mouth. If
anyone popped
their head round
the door, the troll
would roar and
rumble and threaten to
tear them to pieces.

One time, just as the folk were leaving
the farm, there came a man with a
performing bear. They told him about the
troll and advised him to get away from
there. But the man was looking for shelter
and begged to be allowed to stay. He was

determined, so they finally gave him leave.

Towards the evening, the troll came to the farm with his sack on his back. He sat down by the fire, opened the sack and pulled out one toad after another. He took each one by its hind legs and held it over the fire till it was roasted, and then swallowed it. So one toad after the other went inside him for some time.

Then the troll turned to the man and, pointing to the bear, said, "What's your beast's name?"

"Toad," said the man.

The troll took a toad, roasted it and held it out to the bear, saying, "Toad shall have a toad." But as he did so, the man pinched the bear's arm and the bear growled and began to rise.

The Troll and the Bear

"Just you take care," said the man to the troll, "don't make him angry or he'll tear you into pieces."

The troll looked quite frightened and asked, "More like him?"

"No," said the man, "all the others are much bigger and fiercer than him."

"Where others?" said the troll.

"Oh," said the man. "They're coming up the hillside looking for their food."

The troll made haste to tie up the toads he had left in the sack. Then he threw it on his back and went out the door in a hurry.

Next morning, when the people of the farm came home, the man was lying in the bed and the bear beside the fire, both quite comfortable. When the man told them how he had got on they were very glad, and told

The Troll and the Bear

him to come again next Christmas Eve. He did, but the troll did not come, and has never shown himself there since.

The Nix in Mischief

Mrs Ewing

A nix is a water goblin, or sprite,
that appears in many German folk tales.

A certain lake in Germany was once the home of a nix, who became tired of life underwater and decided to go into the upper world to amuse himself.

His friends and relations all tried to persuade him not to go. "Be wise," they said, "and remain where you are safe. You have no reason to leave the lake. Few of our kind have had dealings with the human race without suffering from their curiosity or clumsiness. Do them what good you may, but in the long run you won't get thanked for your deeds. Think how many lakes they have already banished us from. Leave them well alone and stay where you are."

But this advice did not please the nix and he only said, "I shall not expect gratitude, but I wish to amuse myself. The dwarves and goblins play whatever pranks they please on men and women and they do not always have the worst of it. When I hear of their adventures the soles of my feet tingle. Am I to be left out of the fun because I live in a lake instead of a hill?"

His friends repeated their warnings, but

the nix didn't listen. He spent his time dreaming of the clever tricks by which he should outwit the human race.

Shortly after this, a young girl came down to the lake to gather water to wash with. She dipped her pail in just above the nix's

head and in a moment he jumped in, and
was carried safely to land.

The maid was Bess, the washerwoman's
daughter. As she had had one good scolding
that morning for oversleeping, and another
about noon for being slow with her work,
she took up the pail and set off home
without delay.

Though she held it steadily enough, the
bucket shook and the water spilled out.
Thinking that her right arm might be tired,
she moved the weight to her left but with
no better success. The water still spilled out
at every step. "One would think there were
fishes in the pail," Bess said, as she set it
down. But there was nothing to be seen but
a thin, red water worm wriggling at the
bottom. It was in this shape that the nix had

disguised himself, and he almost wriggled out of his skin with delight at the success of his first attempt at mischief.

When they went forward once more, the nix leapt and jumped harder than ever, so that not only was the water spilled, but the girl's dress was soaked.

"The pail is bewitched!" cried the poor girl. "How my mother will scold me for this! My back aches as if I were carrying lead, and yet the water is nearly all gone."

"This is something like fun!" laughed the nix, and by the time they came to their journey's end, there was only a tiny bit of water in the pail.

"Was there ever a poor woman cursed with such a careless daughter?" cried the mother when she saw the dripping dress.

The Nix in Mischief

Meanwhile, the nix could hardly stop laughing. When the woman told Bess to warm some water quickly for the wash, he was in no way worried. He had never seen boiling water, and he slipped from the pail into the kettle.

"Now," cried the mother sharply, "see if you can lift that kettle without slopping water all over your clothes."

"Aye, aye," laughed the nix, "see if you can, my dear!" As poor Bess seized it in her sturdy red hands, he began to dance as before. But the kettle had a lid, which the pail had not. Bess was a strong, strapping lass and with an effort she set the kettle on the fire. "I shall be glad when I'm safely in bed," she muttered. "Everything has gone wrong today."

"It is warm in here," said the nix to himself after a while. "In fact – stuffy. But one must pay something for a frolic, and it tickles my ears to hear that old woman scolding her daughter for my pranks. It is worth a little discomfort, though it certainly is warm, and I think it is growing warmer."

The bottom of the kettle grew quite hot and burned the nix so that he had to jump up and down in the water to keep himself cool. The noise of this made the woman think that the kettle was boiling, and she began to scold her daughter as before, shouting, "Are you coming with that kettle tonight or not? The water is hot already."

This time the nix laughed (as they say) on the other side of his face, for the water had now become as hot as the bottom of the kettle, and he screamed at the top of his shrill tiny voice with pain.

"How the kettle sings tonight!" said Bess, "And how it rains!" she added. For at that moment a tremendous storm burst around the house and rain poured down in sheets of water, as if it meant to wash everything into the lake.

The kettle now really boiled and the lid danced up and down with the frantic leaping and jumping of the nix, who puffed and blew till his breath came out of the spout in clouds of steam.

"If your eyes were as sharp as your ears you'd see that the water is boiling over," snapped the woman. Giving her daughter a passing push, she hurried to the fireplace and lifted the kettle onto the ground.

But no sooner had she set it down, than the lid flew off and out jumped a little green water goblin. The nix ran straight out of the door, wringing his hands and crying, "Three hundred and three years have I lived in the water of this lake and I never knew it to boil before!"

As he crossed the threshold, a clap of thunder broke with what sounded like a peal of laughter from many voices, and then the storm stopped as suddenly as it had begun.

The woman now saw what had happened. The next morning she did not fail to fasten an old horseshoe to the door of her house to keep the nixes out in future. And seeing that she had been unfair to her daughter, she bought her the prettiest set of pink ribbons that were to be found at the next fair.

Bess (who wasn't much bothered by a few sharp scoldings) thought this was the best bargain she had ever made. But whether the nix was equally well satisfied is not known.

The Widow's Son

Katharine Pyle

A Scandinavian tale

Once upon a time a poor lad set out to earn his living. He journeyed on a short way and a long way, and then came to a dark and gloomy wood. The lad had not gone far into it when he met a tall troll, as dark and gloomy as the wood itself, who said, "What are you doing here?"

"I am seeking work," answered the widow's son.

The Widow's Son

"Then come with me and I will give you enough to do but not too much," said the troll. They set out and travelled along, and after a while they came to a great, dark house set all alone in the midst of the wood. The troll showed the lad in and told him what to do.

The lad worked hard and pleased his new master, so after a few days the troll said, "I am going away on a journey. Until I return you may do as you please. But there is one part of the house you have never seen, and that is the three cellars. If you so much as open one of the doors, you will suffer for it."

"Why should I want to go into the cellars?" asked the lad. "The house and the yard are good enough for me."

The lad stayed at the house, and cleaned

and polished and ate and drank. 'I wonder what can be in those cellars that my master does not want me to see,' thought the lad. 'Not that I mean to look, but it does no harm to wonder about it.'

Every hour that the lad stayed there in the house alone he grew more curious about the cellars. At last he could bear it no longer. "I'll just take a wee peep into one of them," he said. "That can surely do no harm to anyone."

So he opened the cellar door and went down a flight of stone steps into the first cellar. He looked all about him. There was nothing at all there but a whip made of thorns lying on a shelf behind the door. "That is not much for the master to have made such a fuss about," said the lad.

The Widow's Son

Then he went on to the second cellar. He opened the door and looked about, but all he saw was a shelf behind the door, and on it was a water jug.

"There is not much to see and I wish I had not come," said the lad to himself.

Next he opened the third door and there was a magnificent coal-black horse chained to a manger, and the manger was filled with red-hot coals. At the horse's tail was a basket of hay.

"That is a cruel thing to do to an animal," cried the lad. He untied the horse from the manger and turned him so he could eat.

Then the black horse spoke to him in a human voice. "You have done a kind act," said the horse, "and you shall not suffer for it. If the Troll Master finds you here when he returns he will surely take your life, and that must not be. Promise to do exactly what I say and you shall be safe. Take the thorn whip and the jug of water. Then mount my back and ride. If the Troll Master finds us here when he returns, it will be terrible for both of us."

The lad did as the horse told him. He took the thorn whip and the jug of water, and mounted the black horse's back. The horse carried him up the steps, out of the house and fast, fast away through the forest and over the plains beyond.

After a while the black horse said, "I hear a noise behind us. Look and see whether anyone is coming."

The lad turned and looked. "Yes, yes, it is the master," he said, "and with him is a whole crowd of people."

"They are his troll friends," said the horse. "Throw the thorn whip behind us, but be

sure you throw it clear and do not let it touch even the tip of my tail."

The lad threw the thorn whip behind him and at once a great forest of thorns grew up

The Widow's Son

where it fell. No one could have forced a way through it. The troll and his friends had to go home and get clubs and axes to cut a path through.

By this time the horse had gone a long, long way. Then he said to the lad, "Look back and see whether you see anyone, for I hear a noise behind us."

The lad looked back. "I see the master coming," he said, "and a great number of monsters with him."

"Yes, yes," said the horse. "He has all of his friends with him now. We must not let them catch us. Pour the water from the jug behind us, but be careful that none of it touches me."

The lad stretched back his arm and poured the water out from the jug, but his haste was such that three drops fell upon the horse's flanks. Immediately a great lake rose about them, and because of the three drops that had fallen on the horse, the lake was not only behind them but about them, and the horse had to swim for it.

The trolls came to the edge of the lake. As there was no way to cross over, they threw themselves down on their stomachs and began to drink it up. They drank and they drank and they drank, until at last they all burst.

The horse went on until he came to a wood and there he stopped. "Get down now," he said to the lad, "then take your sword and cut off my head."

The Widow's Son

When the lad heard this he was horrified.
"What is this you ask of me?" he cried. "All
that I have I owe to you. How could I in
return do you such an injury?"

But the black horse reminded the lad that
he had promised. The youth could not
refuse after that. He drew his sword and cut
off the horse's head. At once, instead of a
coal-black horse, a handsome young prince
stood before him. The lad could barely
believe his eyes. He stared about him,
wondering what had become of the horse.

"There is no need to look for the black
horse," said the stranger, "for I am he." He
then told the lad that he was the son of the
king of a neighbouring country. An enemy
had risen up and slain the king, and had
given the prince to the troll, who had

turned him into a horse and taken him away to his castle. "You have rescued me from the enchantment and now I am free to claim my land again," said the prince.

After that the lad and the prince rode to the prince's own country. His people received him with joy, and he and the lad lived in the greatest friendship forever after.

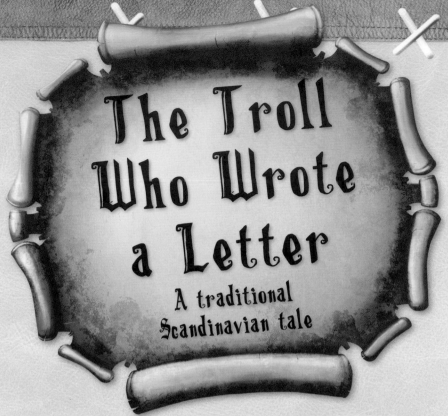

The Troll
Who Wrote
a Letter

A traditional
Scandinavian tale

Once upon a time a troll set up his home near the village of Kund, in a high bank where he had scrabbled out a cave to live in. However the people of the village, not knowing he was there, built a church on the land above his bank. This made the old troll very cross. The bells ringing in the steeple at all hours and the bustle of people coming and going from the church troubled him dreadfully. All trolls hate the sound of bells ringing. In the end he decided to leave his home and find one in some country without any village or church.

The troll travelled out into the wilds where he made his home among the swamps and bushes. But he hated the people of Kund for forcing him out of his home.

Now, a man who had lately settled in the village of Kund came past the swamp and met this troll on the road. It was late at night and he didn't notice that the troll was not a man like himself.

"Where do you live?" asked the troll.

The man answered him truthfully and said, "I am from the town of Kund."

The troll had been waiting for a chance like this to get his revenge on the village.

"So," said the troll, "I don't know you then. And yet I think I know every man in Kund. Will you be so kind as to take a letter for me back with you to Kund?"

The man said he would gladly do so. The troll took a letter out of his pocket and said, "I beg you then, to take this letter to

The Troll Who Wrote a Letter

Kund, not removing it from your pocket until you get there. And when you get there, throw it over the churchyard wall. The person it is for will expect it there."

'What a strange way to deliver a letter' thought the man. But he agreed to do what he was asked.

The troll then went away in great haste, and with him the letter went entirely out of the man's mind. But when he was halfway along the road, the man sat down by the meadow where Tiis lake now is to eat his bread and cheese. He suddenly remembered the troll's letter and the strange instructions that went with it. He felt a great curiosity to look at the letter, even though he had promised not to take it out of his pocket.

'I won't open it' he thought, 'but no harm

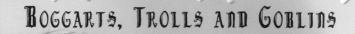

can come from just
looking at the outside.'

So he took the letter out of his pocket
and sat a while with it in his hands.
Suddenly a little water began to dribble out
from beneath the seal. The letter now
unfolded itself and the water came out faster
and faster, pouring in great waves out of the

The Troll Who Wrote a Letter

letter. The poor man had to scramble for his life, and only just got away safely. The wicked troll, hoping to drown the church, had enclosed a whole lake in the letter.

The troll had thought he would get revenge on Kund church by destroying it in this way. But God ordered it so that the lake ran out in the great meadow, where Tiis lake now stands.

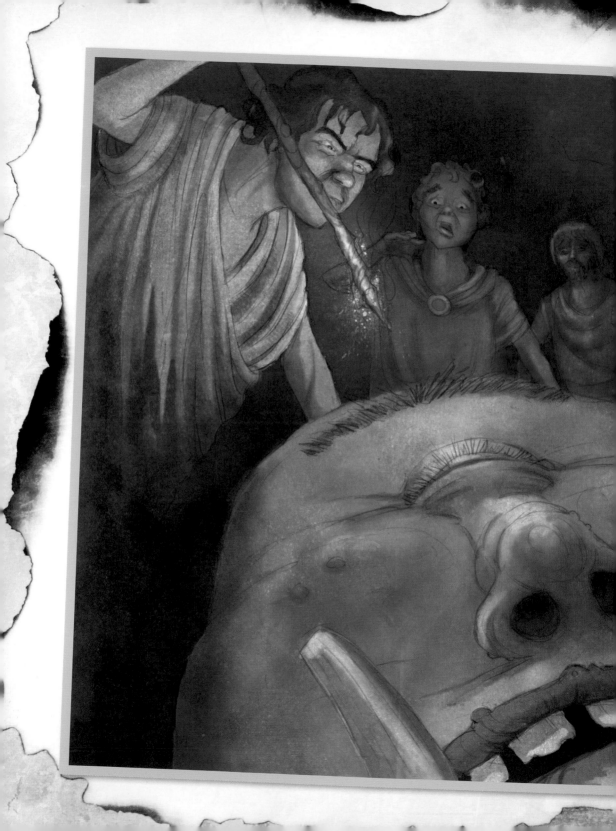

Gruesome Giants and Awful Ogres

Giant Tom and Giant Blubb 210

Buchettino 220

Brabo and the Giant 228

Odysseus and the Cyclops 236

Jack in Wales 248

The Three Little Pigs and the Ogre 256

Thor's Adventures among the Giants 270

Momotaro 282

Thirteenth 288

The Giant of the Flood 297

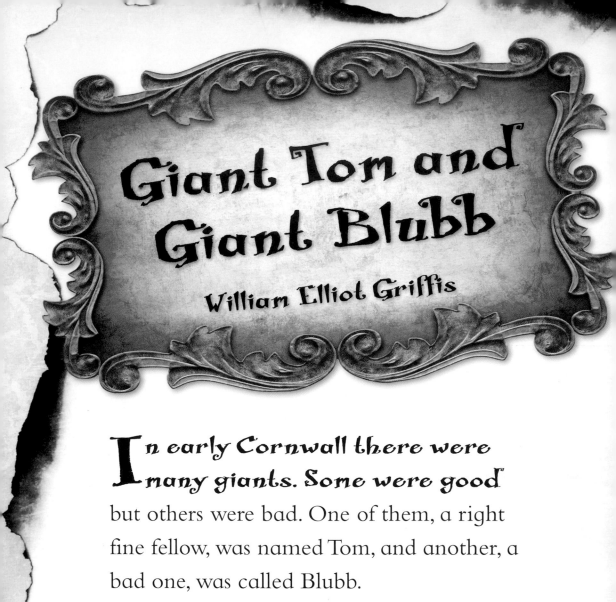

Giant Tom and Giant Blubb

William Elliot Griffis

In early Cornwall there were many giants. Some were good but others were bad. One of them, a right fine fellow, was named Tom, and another, a bad one, was called Blubb.

This bad giant had had twenty wives and was awfully cruel. Nobody ever knew what became of the twenty maidens he had married. Sometimes people called this big fellow Giant Blunderbuss, but Blubb was his name for short. He was mostly made up of head and stomach, for his main thought was to eat. His skull was as big as a market wagon loaded with carrots, but most people believed a coconut would hold all the brains he had.

Giant Blubb had built a mighty castle between a big hill and a river. Under it were cellars of great size filled with treasures of many kinds – gold, silver, jewels and gems. To guard his underground treasures, Giant Blubb had two huge and fierce dogs, supposed to be named Catchem and Tearem. But the names their master really called them by was a secret. Yet anyone who had a piece of meat ready to throw to them and knew their real names, which were passwords, could quieten them. Then they could walk right by the dogs and get the treasures.

Besides these dogs, the only living thing in the castle when the giant went out was the latest Mrs Blubb. Yet she was in constant fear for her life, thinking that her big husband would make a meal out of her sometime soon.

What made all the country hate this cruel giant was not just his awful appetite. It was because he had ruined the King's Highway. When Giant Blubb wanted to make his castle bigger, he had the walls and towers built down to the river's edge. This closed off the highway so that people had to go far around and up over the hill, or by boat along the river. Such a round about way took much time and trouble for all.

Everybody had to put up with it until Giant Tom came along. His real name was Rolling Stone, for he never stuck long in one place at a job and didn't care for money or fine clothes.

This jolly fellow was very good-natured and popular, but often lazy. However, as he could do six men's work when he put his mind to it – as often he did – he was always welcome. In fact, he was too popular for his own good.

One day, when ten fellows were trying to lift a big, long log onto a cart and were unable to do it, Tom came along and told

them to stand back. Then he hoisted the log
onto the cart, roped it into place and told
the cartman to drive on. All the fellows
cheered him and one of them lifted his cap
and cried out, "Hurrah for Giant Tom. He's
the fellow to whip Giant Blubb."

"He is! He is!" they all cried
out in chorus.

"Who is this Giant Blubb?
Where does he live?" asked
Tom, rolling up his sleeves.

Then they told Tom the
story of how the big bully
had ruined the King's
Highway by building a great
wall and tower across the
road to shut it off.

"Never mind, boys. I'll see to

him," said Tom. "Leave the matter with me."

The next day, Giant Tom went into town and hired himself out to drive a wagon. He asked the boss to give him the route that led past Giant Blubb's castle, over the King's Highway.

The boss said, "Go ahead, my boy. I'll pay you double wages if you will open that road again."

Tom drove off. He occupied all the room on the seat of the cart, which two men usually filled and left plenty of room on either side.

Cracking his whip, the driver kept the four horses at a galloping pace. Very soon he called out, "Whoa," before the curved high gateway of Giant Blubb.

Tom shouted from the depth of his lungs,

"Open the gate and let me drive through. This is the King's Highway."

For a minute, the only reply was the barking of the dogs. Then a rattling of bolts was heard and the great gates swung open.

"Who are you, you rude fellow? Go round over the hill or I'll thrash you," shouted Giant Blubb in a rage.

"Better save your breath, you big boaster, and come out and fight," said Tom.

"Fight? You dwarf. I'll just get a stick and whip you, as I would a bad boy."

Giant Blubb stepped aside into the grove nearby, all the while keeping an eye on his gate, guarded by his two monstrous dogs. He chose an elm tree twenty feet high, tore it up by the roots, pulled off the branches and peeled it for a whip. Meanwhile, Giant

Giant Tom and Giant Blubb

Tom turned over the wagon, pulled out its longest plank and took off one of the wheels. Then, as if armed with a spear and shield, he advanced to meet Giant Blubb. Giant Tom whistled like a boy as he marched forwards.

Giant Blubb lifted his elm whip to strike,

but Tom warded off the blow with his wheel shield. Then he punched him in the stomach with the plank, so hard that the big fellow slipped and rolled over in the mud.

Picking himself up, Giant Blubb, now half blind with rage, rushed towards Giant Tom, who, this time, made a lunge that knocked Giant Blubb over.

But Tom was not a cruel fellow and had no desire to kill anyone. So he threw down his plank and wheel.

But instead of thanking Tom, Giant Blubb rushed at him again. He was in too much of a rage to see anything clearly, while Tom, perfectly cool, gave the angry giant a kick in the stomach. Giant Blubb fell down again and rolled on the ground. Then Tom sent the giant on his way.

Giant Tom and Giant Blubb

Tom made himself owner of Giant Blubb's castle and all its treasures. He opened the King's Highway again, made sure his aging mother had all she needed, and was always kind to the sick and poor.

In Cornwall today, they still tell stories of the big fellow who got rid of Giant Blubb's gate.

Buchettino

Thomas Frederick Crane

Once upon a time there was a child whose name was Buchettino. One morning his mamma called him and said, "Buchettino, will you do me a favour? Go and sweep the stairs." Buchettino, who was very obedient, did not wait to be told a second time, but went at once to sweep the stairs.

After sweeping all around, he found a

penny. Then he said to himself, "What shall I do with this penny? I have half a mind to buy some dates… but no! For I should have to throw away the stones. I will buy some apples… no! I will not, for I should have to throw away the core. I will buy some nuts… but no! For I should have to throw away the shells. What shall I buy, then? I will buy – I will buy – enough! I will buy a pennyworth of figs."

No sooner said than done. Buchettino bought a pennyworth of figs and went and sat up in a tree to eat them. While he was eating, an ogre passed by. Seeing Buchettino eating figs in the tree, the ogre said, "Buchettino, my dear Buchettino, give me a little fig with your dear little hand. If you don't, I will eat you!"

Buchettino threw the ogre a fig, but it fell in the dirt. The ogre repeated, "Buchettino, my dear Buchettino, give me a little fig with your dear little hand. If you don't, I will eat you!"

Then Buchettino threw him another, which also fell in the dirt. The ogre said again, "Buchettino, my dear Buchettino, give me a little fig with your dear little

Buchettino

hand. If you don't, I will eat you!"

Poor Buchettino. He did not see the trick and did not know that the ogre was trying to get him into his bag and eat him up.

What does Buchettino do? He leans down and foolishly gives the ogre a fig with his little hand.

The ogre, who wanted nothing better, suddenly grabbed Buchettino by the arm and put him into his bag. Then he put the bag on his back and headed for his home, crying, "Wife, my wife, put the kettle on the fire, for I have caught Buchettino! Wife, my wife, put the kettle on the fire, for I have caught Buchettino!"

When the ogre was near his house he put the bag on the ground and went off to attend to something else. Buchettino, with a knife that he had in his pocket, cut the bag open in a moment, filled it with large stones and then said, "My legs, run away for we need to go."

When the rascal of an ogre returned he picked up the bag and scarcely had he arrived home when he said to his wife, "Tell me, my wife, have you put the kettle on the fire?" She answered at once, "Yes."

"Then," said the ogre, "we will cook Buchettino. Come here and help me." Taking the bag, they carried it to the hearth to throw poor Buchettino into the kettle, but instead they found only the

Buchettino

stones. Imagine how cheated the ogre felt. He was so angry that he bit his hands. The ogre could not bear the thought of losing Buchettino, and he swore to find him again and get his revenge.

So the next day, the ogre began to go all about the city and to look in all the hiding places. At last he happened to raise his eyes and saw Buchettino on a balcony, laughing so hard that his mouth stretched from ear to ear. The ogre thought he should burst with rage, but he pretended not to be angry and in a very sweet tone he said, "Buchettino, tell me, how did you manage to climb up there?"

Buchettino answered, "Do you really want to know? Then listen. I put dishes upon dishes, glasses upon glasses, pans upon

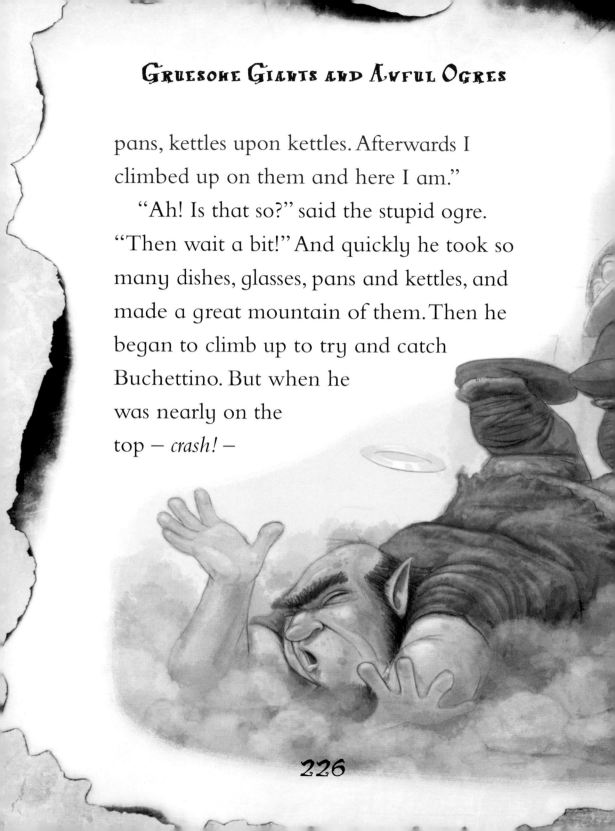

pans, kettles upon kettles. Afterwards I climbed up on them and here I am."

"Ah! Is that so?" said the stupid ogre. "Then wait a bit!" And quickly he took so many dishes, glasses, pans and kettles, and made a great mountain of them. Then he began to climb up to try and catch Buchettino. But when he was nearly on the top — *crash!* —

Buchettino

everything fell down. That rascal of an
ogre fell down on the stones and was
cheated again. The ogre was so
cross he went off to another
country and never troubled
Buchettino again.

Then Buchettino, very
pleased with himself, ran
home to his mamma.

Brabo and the Giant

William Elliot Griffis

Ages ago, when the giants were numerous on the earth, there lived a big fellow named Antigonus. This giant was rough and cruel. He built a strong castle on the Scheldt River in Belgium, where the city of Antwerp now stands. The castle had four sides and high walls, and deep down in the earth were dark, damp dungeons.

Brabo and the Giant

Now, the river on which the giant built his castle was very grand, deep and wide. The captains of ships liked to sail on it because there was no danger from rocks and the country through which it flowed was so pretty.

Every day, one could see hundreds of white-sailed craft moving towards the sea or coming in from the ocean. The incoming ships brought sugar, wine, oranges, lemons, olives and other good things to eat, and wool to make warm clothes.

But one day, the wicked giant came into the country to stop the ships and make the captains pay him money. He strode through the town with a big knotted club made out of an oak tree. He cried out to all the people to assemble in the great open square.

"From this day forth," he roared, "no ship shall pass by this place without my permission. Every captain must pay me. Whoever refuses shall have both his hands cut off and thrown into the river."

With this, the giant swung and twirled his club in the air and

then brought it down on a poor countryman's cart, smashing it into pieces.

Now, there was a brave young fellow named Brabo, who lived in the province of Brabant. He studied the giant's castle and saw a window where he could climb up and get into the giant's chamber.

Brabo went to the Duke and promised that if his lord's soldiers would storm the gates of the castle, he would seek out and fight the giant. While the soldiers battered down the gates, he would climb the walls. "He's nothing but a bully and a boaster," said Brabo.

The Duke agreed. On a dark night, one thousand of his best men-at-arms marched towards the giant's castle, but with no drums or trumpets or anything that could make a noise.

Reaching a wood full of big trees near the castle, Brabo and the soldiers waited till after midnight. All the dogs in the town and country for five miles around were seized and put into barns, so as not to bark and wake the giant up. They were given plenty to eat, so they quickly fell asleep and were perfectly quiet.

At the given signal, hundreds of men holding ships' masts or tree trunks marched against the castle gates. They punched and pounded, and at last smashed the iron-bound timbers and rushed in. At about the same time, the barn doors where the dogs had been kept were thrown open. In full cry, hundreds of the animals, from puppies to hounds, were at once out, barking, howling and yelping, as if they knew what was going on and wanted to see the fun.

But where was the giant? None of the captains could find him. Not one of the prisoners held in the castle or the soldiers could tell where he had hidden.

Brabo was not afraid. Some of his comrades outside helped him to set up a tall ladder against the wall. Then, while all the watchers and men-at-arms had gone to defend the gates, Brabo climbed into the castle through a slit in the thick wall. This had been cut out, like a window, for the bow-and-arrow men. Sword in hand, Brabo made for the giant's own room.

Glaring at the youth, the big fellow seized his club and brought it down with such force that it went through the wooden floor. But Brabo dodged the blow and, in a moment, made a sweep with his sword. Cutting off the giant's head, he threw it out the window. It had hardly touched the ground before the dogs arrived. One of the largest of these ran away with the trophy, and the big, ugly head of the bully was never found again.

Very soon, every house in Antwerp displayed lighted candles and the city was lit up. After this, thousands of ships from many countries loaded and unloaded their cargoes at the quays or sailed peacefully by.

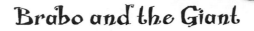

Brabo and the Giant

Antwerp became rich again. The people loved their native city so dearly that they made the proverb: 'All the world is a ring, and Antwerp is the pearl set in it'.

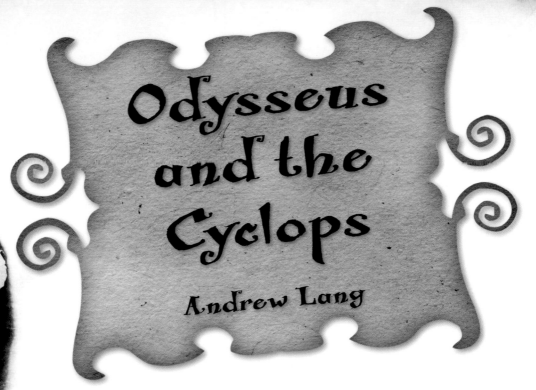

Odysseus and the Cyclops

Andrew Lang

The Greek hero, Odysseus, is sailing with his men back from Troy to his own country. They have stopped at an island to get food and water.

When they were near the shore they saw a great cave by the sea. It was roofed in with green laurel branches, and seemed to be meant as a place to shelter sheep and goats. Round about it a high outer wall was built with stones, and tall, leafy pines and oak trees.

In this cave, all alone with his flocks and herds, lived a huge, hideous Cyclops who was called Polyphemus.

Leaving some of his men to guard the ship, Odysseus took his best warriors with him and went to explore the one-eyed giant's cave. With him he carried a goat-skin full of precious wine that was dark red, sweet and strong.

Soon they came to the cave, but Polyphemus was not there. He had taken his flocks of sheep off to graze in the green meadows, leaving pens full of lambs and kids in the cave.

Towards evening, Polythemus came, driving his flocks before him and carrying a huge load of firewood on his back. He cast

it down on the floor with a thunderous noise. Odysseus and his men fled in fear and hid themselves in the darkest corners of the cave. When Polyphemus had driven his sheep inside, he lifted from the ground a rock so huge that twenty-two four-wheeled wagons could not have carried it. With it, the giant blocked the doorway. Then he lit a fire and, when the flames lit up the dark-walled cave, he spied Odysseus and his men.

"Strangers, who are you?" he asked, in his great, rumbling voice. "Are you merchants or are you sea robbers?"

The sound of the giant's voice and the sight of his hideous face filled the men's hearts with terror, but Odysseus answered, "We come from Troy, driven here by winds and waves."

Polyphemus said nothing in reply, but sprang up and grabbed hold of two of the men. He ate the two men, bones and all, as if he had been a starving lion. When he had finished his meal, he stretched himself on the ground beside his sheep and goats, and slept.

Helpless and horrified, Odysseus and his men had watched the dreadful sight, but when the giant slept they began to make

plans for their escape. All night they thought
what they should do.

The next morning at dawn, Polyphemus
awoke. He lit a fire, milked his flocks and
gave each ewe her lamb. Next, he lifted the
stone from the door, drove the flocks out
and set the stone back again. Then, with a
loud shout, he turned his sheep and goats
towards the hills and left Odysseus and his
remaining men imprisoned in the cave,
plotting and planning how to get away.

At last Odysseus thought of a plan. By
the sheep pen there lay a huge club of
green olive wood, which Polyphemus had
cut and was keeping until it should be dry
enough to use as a staff. From this club,
Odysseus cut a large piece and gave it to
his men to fine down and make smooth.

Odysseus and the Cyclops

While they did this, Odysseus himself sharpened it to a point and hardened the point in the fire.

When the stake was ready, they hid it among the rubbish on the floor of the cave. In the evening, Polyphemus came down from the hills with his flocks and drove them all inside the cave. From the shadows of the cave Odysseus stepped forwards, holding in his hands an ivy bowl full of the dark red, sweet wine.

"Drink wine," said Odysseus, "and see what drink we carried on our ship."

Polyphemus quickly gulped down the strong wine.

"Give me more," he cried. "And tell me your name, stranger."

Again and again, Odysseus gave him the

bowl full of wine, until the strong wine went to the giant's head and made him stupid.

Then Odysseus said, "You asked me my name. Noman is my name, and Noman is what they call me."

The giant answered, "I will eat your friends first, Noman, and you last of all. That shall be my thanks for the wine."

Soon the wine made the giant so sleepy that he sank backwards with his great face upturned and fell fast asleep.

As soon as the giant slept, Odysseus thrust the stake he had prepared into the fire to make it red-hot. Then he drew the red-hot stake out and thrust it into the giant's eye.

With a great and terrible cry the giant sprang to his feet, and

Odysseus and the Cyclops

Odysseus and the others ran to hide. Mad with pain, he called to the other one-eyed giants, who lived in their caves on the hilltops. The giants, hearing his horrid yells, rushed to help him.

"What is the trouble, Polyphemus?" they asked. "Who is hurting or killing you?"

From the other side of the great stone Polyphemus shouted out, "Noman is hurting me."

Then the one-eyed giants said, "If no man is hurting you, then it must be an illness that makes you cry so loud, and this you must bear by yourself, for we cannot help you."

With that they strode away from the cave and left the blind giant groaning and roaring with pain. Groping with his hands,

Odysseus and the Cyclops

Polyphemus found the great stone that blocked the door. He lifted it away and sat himself down in the mouth of the cave with his arms stretched out. Sitting there, he fell asleep and, as soon as he slept, Odysseus planned and plotted how best to escape.

The rams of the giant's flocks were great, strong beasts, with thick and woolly fleeces. Odysseus tied them together in threes, and under the middle ram of each three, he tied one of his men. For himself, he kept the best ram of the flock. Odysseus curled himself underneath this ram and clung to it, his face upwards.

When dawn came, the rams went out of the cave door to the hills and green meadows. As each sheep passed Polyphemus, he felt along its back, but never guessed that the remaining men were bound beneath the thick-fleeced rams. Last of all came the young ram to which Odysseus clung.

The ram slowly walked on past the savage giant, towards the meadows near the sea. And soon they were far enough from the cave for Odysseus to let go of the ram and to stand up.

"There is no time to weep," said Odysseus, and he made his men hurry on board the ship, driving the giant's sheep before them.

Soon they were all on board, and the grey sea water was rushing off their oars as they sailed away very quickly from the land of the one-eyed giants.

Their hearts were sore because they had

Odysseus and the Cyclops

lost brave men of their company, but they were also glad that men had been saved from death at the hands of the Cyclops.

Jack in Wales

Flora Annie Steel

Once upon a time, Jack, the
famous Giant Killer, found
himself lost in wild Wales, far from any
human house. As night fell he wandered on,
until, on entering a narrow valley, he came
to a very large, dreary-looking house,
almost a castle, standing alone.

Being anxious for shelter Jack went up
to the door and knocked. You may

imagine his surprise and alarm when the summons was answered by a giant with two heads. But though this giant's look was very fierce, his manners were quite polite. The truth was that he was an evil giant. He appeared friendly because this was how he tried to win people over, by a show of false friendship.

So he welcomed Jack heartily in a strong Welsh accent and prepared a bedroom for him, where he was left with kind wishes for a good rest.

However, Jack was too tired to sleep well and, as he lay awake, he overheard the giant muttering to himself in the next room. Jack had very keen ears and he was able to make out these words, or something like them:

"Though here you lodge with me
    this night,
You shall not see the morning light.
My club shall dash your brains outright."
    "Do you say!" said Jack,
starting up
at once.

"So that is your trick, is it? But I will be
even with you." Then, leaving his bed, Jack
laid a big piece of wood among the

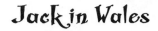

Jack in Wales

blankets and, taking one of these to keep himself warm, made himself snug in a corner of the room. He pretended to snore, so as to make the giant think he was asleep.

And sure enough, in came the giant on tiptoe, carrying a big club. Then –
WHACK! WHACK! WHACK!

Jack could hear the bed being beaten until the giant, thinking every bone of his guest's body must be broken, went out of the room again. Then Jack went calmly to bed once more and slept soundly.

Next morning the giant couldn't believe his eyes when he saw Jack coming down the stairs fresh and hearty.

"Odds splutter hur nails!" he cried astonished. "Did you sleep well? Was there nothing you felt in the night?"

"Oh," replied Jack, laughing in his sleeve, "I think a rat did come and give me two or three flaps of his tail."

The giant was dumbfounded. He led Jack to breakfast, brought him a bowl that held at least four gallons of porridge, and told him to eat the lot.

Jack in Wales

When Jack was travelling he wore a leather bag under his cloak to carry his things and, as it happened, he still had it with him. So, quick as thought, he hitched it round in front with the opening just under his chin.

Then he set to work at the mighty bowl, filled to the brim with grey, lumpy porridge. As he spooned up the mixture, he slipped the best part of it into the leather bag without the giant being any the wiser.

So they sat down to breakfast, the giant gobbling down his own measure of porridge, while Jack carried on with his.

"Now see," says crafty Jack when he had finished. "I'll show you a trick," and with that he stood up with a carving-knife, ripped up the leather bag and out fell all

254

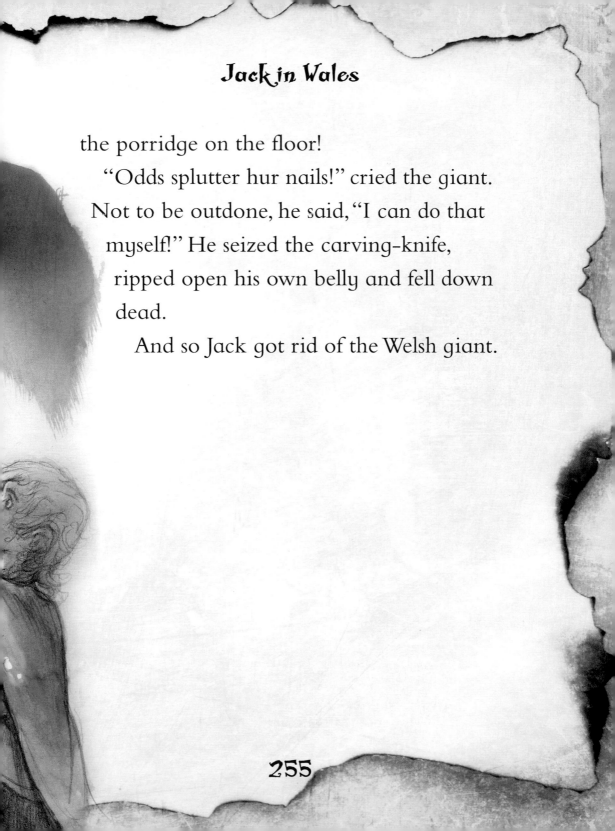

Jack in Wales

the porridge on the floor!

"Odds splutter hur nails!" cried the giant. Not to be outdone, he said, "I can do that myself!" He seized the carving-knife, ripped open his own belly and fell down dead.

And so Jack got rid of the Welsh giant.

The Three Little Pigs and the Ogre

Howard Pyle

There were once three nice, fat little pigs. The first was small, the second was smaller and the third was the smallest of all. These three little pigs thought of going out into the woods to gather acorns, for there were better acorns there than here.

"There's a great ogre who lives over in the woods," said the barnyard cock.

The Three Little Pigs and the Ogre

"And he will eat you up, body and bones," said the speckled hen.

"And that will be the end of you," said the black drake.

"If folks only knew what was good for them, they would stay at home," said the grey goose.

But the smallest of all the little pigs wanted to go out into the woods whether there was an ogre or not. So out into the woods he went.

The smallest little pig hunted for acorns here and there, and who should he meet but the great, wicked ogre himself.

"Aha!" the ogre said, "It is a nice, plump little pig that I have been wanting for my supper these last few days. So you will just come along with me now."

The little pig said he would go, but he asked the ogre if he had come across three fellows tramping about in the woods.

The ogre said he had met nobody in the woods that day.

"Dear, dear," said the smallest little pig, "but that is a pity, for those three fellows were three wicked robbers. They have just hidden a bag full of money in that hole up in the tree."

You can guess how the ogre pricked up his ears at this and how he stared till his eyes were as big as saucers.

"Just wait," said he to the smallest little pig, "I will be down again in a minute." So the ogre laid his jacket to one side and he climbed up the tree, up and up a long way, for he wanted to find that bag of money

The Three Little Pigs and the Ogre

and he meant to keep it.

"Do you see the hole?" said the smallest of the little pigs.

The ogre said he could see the hole.

"And do you see the money?" the smallest of the little pigs asked.

The ogre said he could not see the money.

"Then, goodbye," said the smallest of the little pigs, and off he trotted home, leaving the ogre to climb down the tree.

"At least now you will go out into the woods no more," said the cock, the speckled hen, the black drake and the grey goose.

Well, there was no telling what the three little pigs would do – they would have to wait and see.

Next day, it was the middle-sized little pig who wanted to go out into the woods, for he also wanted to taste the acorns there.

So out into the woods the middle-sized little pig went, and there he had all the acorns that he wanted.

But the ogre came along. "Aha!" he said. "Now I have a plump pig for my supper for sure and certain."

But the middle-sized little pig just stood and looked at a great rock in front of him.

The Three Little Pigs and the Ogre

"Sh-h-h-h-h-h!" he said, "I am not to be talked to or bothered now!"

And why was the middle-sized pig not to be talked to or bothered? That was what the ogre really wanted to know.

The middle-sized little pig said he was looking at what was going on under the great rock, for he could see the little fairy folk brewing more beer than thirty-seven men could drink.

The ogre said he would like to see that for himself.

"Very well," said the middle-sized little pig, "there is nothing easier than to learn that trick. Just take a handful of leaves from that bush and rub them over your eyes. Then shut your eyes tight and count to fifty."

The ogre said he would have a try at
that. So he gathered a handful of the leaves
and rubbed them over
his eyes, just as the
middle-sized
pig had
said.

The Three Little Pigs and the Ogre

"And now are you ready?" said the middle-sized little pig.

The ogre said he was ready.

"Then shut your eyes and count," said the middle-sized little pig.

So the ogre shut his eyes as tightly as he could and began to count, "One, two, three, four, five," and so on. And while he was counting, the little pig was running away home again.

Now it was the largest of the three little pigs who began to talk about going out into the woods to look for acorns.

"You had better stay at home and take things as they come." That was what the cock, the speckled hen, the black drake and the grey goose said.

But the little pig wanted to go out into

the woods, and into the woods the little pig would go, ogre or no ogre.

After he had eaten all of the acorns that he wanted he began to think of

going home again, but just then the ogre came stomping along.

The Three Little Pigs and the Ogre

"Aha!" he said, "You shall just come along home with me and tomorrow you shall be made into sausages! There is to be no trickery this time."

"Come, come!" said the largest little pig, sitting back on his heels and regarding the furious ogre quite calmly. "No need to be so angry. I'm willing to do anything you want. If it is sausages that you're after, maybe I can help you. At the farm is a storehouse filled with more sausages and good things than two men can count. There is a window where you could just squeeze through. Only you must promise to eat what you want and to carry nothing away with you."

Well, the ogre liked the idea of that very much. He promised to eat all he wanted in the storehouse and to take nothing away with him, just as the pig had said. And so off they went together.

They came to the storehouse at the farm, and sure enough, there was a window. It was just large enough for the ogre to squeeze through without a button to spare in the size.

Dear, dear! How the ogre did stuff himself with the sausages and puddings and other good things in the storehouse.

Then the little pig bawled out as loud as he could, "Have you had enough yet?"

"Hush-sh-sh-sh-sh-sh-sh!" said the ogre, "Don't talk so loud, or you'll be rousing the folks and having them about our ears like a hive of bees."

"No," bawled the little pig, louder than

before, "but tell me, have you had enough to eat yet?"

"Yes, yes," said the ogre, "I have had almost enough, only be quiet about it!"

"Very well!" bawled the little pig, as loud as he could, "If you have had enough, and if you have eaten all of the sausages and all of the puddings you can, it is about time that you were going. For here comes the farmer and two of his men to see what all the noise is about."

And sure enough, the farmer and his men were coming as fast as they could.

When the ogre heard them coming, he felt sure that it was time that he must be getting away home again. He tried to get out of the same window that he had got in a little while before. But he had stuffed

himself with so much of the good things that he had swelled, and there he stuck in the storehouse window like a cork in a bottle, and could budge neither one way nor the other.

The Three Little Pigs and the Ogre

"Oho!" said the farmer, "You were after my sausages and my puddings, were you? Then you will come no more."

And that was so, for when the farmer and his men were done with the ogre, he never went into the woods again.

As for the three little pigs, they trotted into the woods every day of their lives, for there was nobody to stop them from gathering all the acorns that they wanted.

Thor's Adventures among the Giants

Julia Goddard

From *Wonderful Stories from Northern Lands*

Thor is the son of Odin, the Norse king of the Gods. Loki is Thor's mischievous companion.

Once upon a time Thor set out upon his travels, taking Loki with him. They set off together in Thor's chariot, drawn by its two strong male goats.

They could just see a dark forest in the far distance. One or two huge rocks and great blocks of stone were scattered about.

Thor's Adventures among the Giants

They pushed on and soon found that they were in a land where no men lived. The darkness became so deep by the time they reached the forest, that they only knew they had arrived there because Loki hit his head against a low branch.

Soon after this, Thor cried out, "Good luck! I have found a house. Follow close after me and we will make ourselves comfortable for the night."

They groped their way along the wall, seeking to find an entrance. At last Thor found a huge entrance opening into a wide hall. Passing through this they turned to the left into a large room that was quite empty. Here, after eating some food, they stretched themselves upon the hard floor and fell asleep.

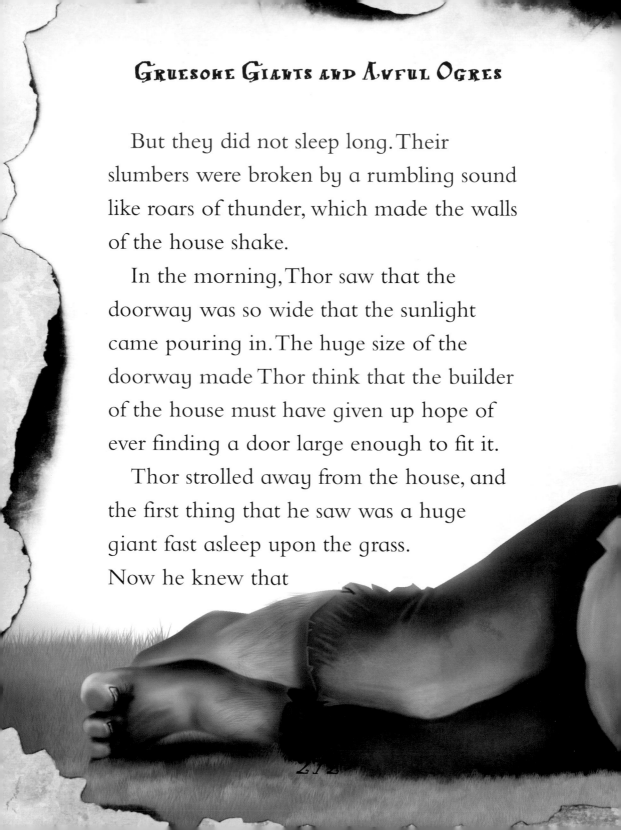

But they did not sleep long. Their slumbers were broken by a rumbling sound like roars of thunder, which made the walls of the house shake.

In the morning, Thor saw that the doorway was so wide that the sunlight came pouring in. The huge size of the doorway made Thor think that the builder of the house must have given up hope of ever finding a door large enough to fit it.

Thor strolled away from the house, and the first thing that he saw was a huge giant fast asleep upon the grass. Now he knew that

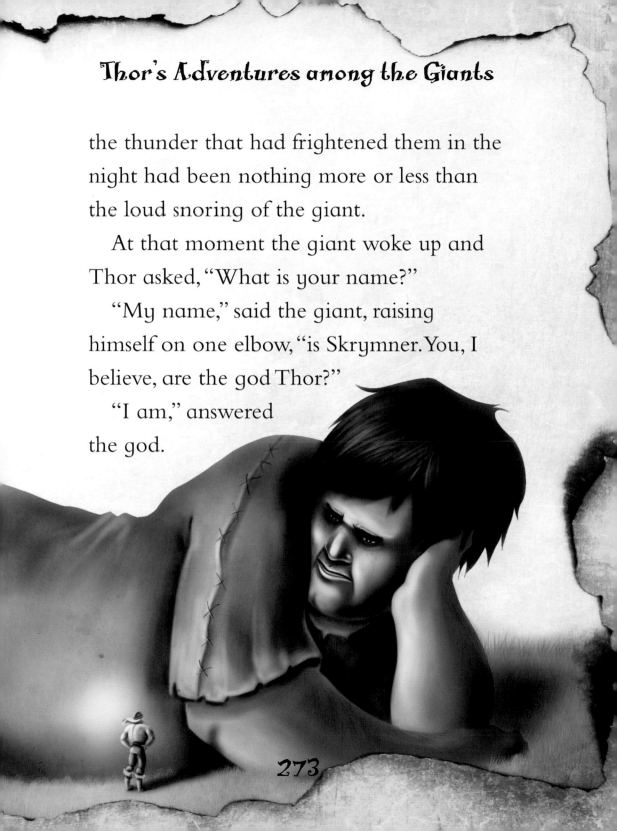

Thor's Adventures among the Giants

the thunder that had frightened them in the night had been nothing more or less than the loud snoring of the giant.

At that moment the giant woke up and Thor asked, "What is your name?"

"My name," said the giant, raising himself on one elbow, "is Skrymner. You, I believe, are the god Thor?"

"I am," answered the god.

273

"Do you happen to have picked up my glove?" asked the giant carelessly.

Then Thor knew that what he and his companion had taken for a large house was only the giant's glove. From this, you can see how huge the giant Skrymner must have been.

Skrymner showed himself to be a kind giant. He insisted upon carrying Thor's bag, putting it into his own wallet, and offered to take Thor and Loki to meet the King.

As they walked, the rising sun fell full upon the city of Utgard, the town of giants, whose huge brass gates glittered in the sunlight. Even though they were so far away, Thor could see how high they were – they made him and his companion seem no larger than grasshoppers.

Thor's Adventures among the Giants

Thor walked on and made his way to the palace. There, he asked to see the King.

After some time Thor was brought before Utgarda Loke, the King of the country. The King had never seen such small men before and there was something so funny in the sight that he burst out laughing.

"Though we are small compared with the giants," said Thor angrily, "we have powers that may surprise you."

"Really!" answered Utgarda Loke, raising his eyebrows. "What can you do?"

"I can drink a wine cup down be it never too big," replied the god.

And then a drinking horn was presented to Thor.

"If you are as great as you pretend to be," said the King, "you will drink it down in one go. Some people take two pulls at it, but the weakest among us can manage it in three."

Thor took up the horn and, being very thirsty, took a steady pull at it. He thought he had done very well but, on removing it from his lips, he was surprised to see how little had gone.

A second time he took a drink, but the horn was far from being emptied.

Again a third time he tried to finish it, but it was almost full to the brim.

"I am disappointed in you," said Utgarda Loke. "You are not half the man I took you for. I see it is no use asking you to do warrior's feats. I must test you in a simpler way. You shall try to lift my cat from the ground."

Thor's Adventures among the Giants

And a large grey cat came leaping along and planted itself firmly before Thor, showing its sharp claws.

Thor seized it, but in spite of all his efforts he was only able to raise one of the cat's paws from the ground.

"Huh!" exclaimed Utgarda Loke, "You are just a baby, fit only for the nursery. I believe that my old nurse, Hela, would be more than a match for you. Hela, come and wrestle with the mighty god Thor."

Out came an old woman. Her eyes were sunken, her arms and legs were thin, and her hair was white as snow.

She came towards Thor and tried to throw him to the ground. Though he put forth his whole strength into the contest, Thor was surprised to find how powerful she was. It needed all his efforts to keep on his feet. For a long time he was successful, but in the end Hela brought him down upon one knee, and Thor had to admit he was conquered.

278

Thor's Adventures among the Giants

Ashamed, he and Loki were making ready to leave the city quietly, when Utgarda Loke sent for them.

He made them a splendid feast and then went with them beyond the city gates.

"Now tell me honestly," said he to Thor, "what do you think of your success?"

"I am astounded and ashamed to be so beaten," replied the god.

"Ha! Ha!" laughed Utgarda Loke. "I knew that you were. However, as we are well out of the city I don't mind telling you a secret or two. The end of the drinking horn, though you did not see it, reached the sea. As fast as you emptied it, it filled again, so that you never could have drained it dry. But the next time that you stand upon the seashore, you will see how much less ocean there is after your large drinking.

"The grey cat was no cat, but the great Serpent of Midgard that twines round the world, and you lifted him so high that we were all quite frightened.

"But your last feat was the most wonderful of all, for Hela was none other than Death. Never did I see anyone before over whom Death had so little power.

"And now, my friend, go on your way and don't come near my city again, for I tell you plainly, I do not want you there. I shall use all kinds of enchantment to keep you out of it."

As he ended his speech, Thor raised his hammer, but Utgarda Loke had vanished.

"I will return to the city," said Thor.

But the giant city was nowhere to be

seen. A pasture spread itself out around him.

So Thor and his companion, thinking about their wonderful adventures, turned their steps towards home.

Momotaro

John Finnemore

A traditional Japanese folk tale

Once upon a time an old man and an old woman lived near a river at the foot of a mountain. Everyday the old man went to the mountain to cut wood and carry it home, while the old woman went to the river to wash clothes.

Now, the old woman was very unhappy because she had no children. It seemed to her that if she only had a son or a daughter

Momotaro

she would be the most fortunate old woman in the world.

One day she was washing the clothes in the river, when she saw something floating down the stream towards her. It was a great peach, and she seized it and carried it home.

As she carried it she heard a sound like the cry of a child. She looked right and left, up and down, but no child was to be seen. She heard the cry again, and now she thought that it came from the big peach. So she cut the peach open at once and, to her great surprise and delight, she found that there was a baby sitting in the middle of it.

She took the child and brought him up, and because he was born in a peach she called him Momotaro, which means 'son of a peach'.

Momotaro grew up a strong, fine boy, and when he was seventeen years old he went out to seek his fortune. He had made up his mind to attack an island where a dreadful ogre lived.

The old woman gave Momotaro plenty of food to eat on the way – corn and rice wrapped in a bamboo leaf, and many other things – and away he went. He had not gone far when he met a wasp.

"Give me a share of your food, Momotaro," said the wasp, "and I will go with you and help you to overcome the dreadful ogre."

Momotaro

"With all my heart," said Momotaro, and he shared his food at once with the wasp.

Soon he met a crab, and the same agreement was made, and then with a chestnut, and last of all with a millstone.

So now the five companions journeyed on together towards the island of the ogre. When they reached the island they crept up to the house of the ogre and found that he was not in his room. So they soon made a plan to take advantage of his absence.

The chestnut laid itself down in the ash of a charcoal fire that had been burning on the hearth, the crab hid himself in a washing pan nearly full of water, the wasp settled in a dusky corner, the millstone climbed onto the roof, and Momotaro hid himself outside.

Before long the ogre came back, and he went to the fire to warm his hands. The chestnut quickly cracked in the hot ashes and threw burning cinders over the ogre's hands. The ogre at once ran to the washing pan, and thrust his hands into it to cool them. The crab caught his fingers and pinched them till the ogre roared with pain. Snatching his hands out of the pan, the ogre leapt into the dusky corner as a safe place. But the wasp came and met him and stung him dreadfully.

In great fright and

Momotaro

misery, the ogre tried to run out of the room, but down came the millstone with a crash on his head and killed him at once.

So, without any trouble to himself, and with the help of his faithful friends, which he had made through his kindness, Momotaro got all the ogre's gold and his fortune was made.

Thirteenth

Thomas Frederick Crane

There was once a father who had thirteen sons, the youngest of whom was named Thirteenth. The father had hard work to support his children, but he made what little money he could gathering herbs.

One day, the King sent out a notice in the city that the person who would go and steal the ogre's bed covering would receive

Thirteenth

a reward of gold. Thirteenth's brothers went
to the King and said, "Majesty, we have a
brother named Thirteenth, who is bold
enough to do that and other things too."

The king said, "Bring him to me at once."

They brought Thirteenth, who said,
"Majesty, how is it possible to steal the ogre's
bed covering? If he sees me he will eat me!"

"No matter, you must go," said the King.
"I know that you are bold."

So Thirteenth went to the house of the
ogre, who was away. The ogress was in the
kitchen. Thirteenth entered quietly and hid
himself under the bed. At night, the ogre
returned. He ate his supper and went to bed,
saying as he did so, "I smell the smell of
human flesh. When I see it, I will eat it!"

The ogress replied, "Be still, no one has

entered here." The ogre began to snore, and Thirteenth pulled the bed covering a little. But the ogre woke up and called out, "What is that?" Thirteenth began to mew like a cat. The ogress said, "Scat! Scat!" and clapped her hands. She then fell asleep again with the ogre. Thirteenth gave a hard pull, seized the bed covering and ran away.

The King was so pleased with the bed covering that he issued another notice: he would give a measure of gold to whoever brought him the ogre's pillow. Thirteenth said, "Majesty, how is that possible? The pillow is full of little bells, and you must know that the ogre awakens at the slightest breath."

"I know nothing about it," said the king. "I just want to have the pillow."

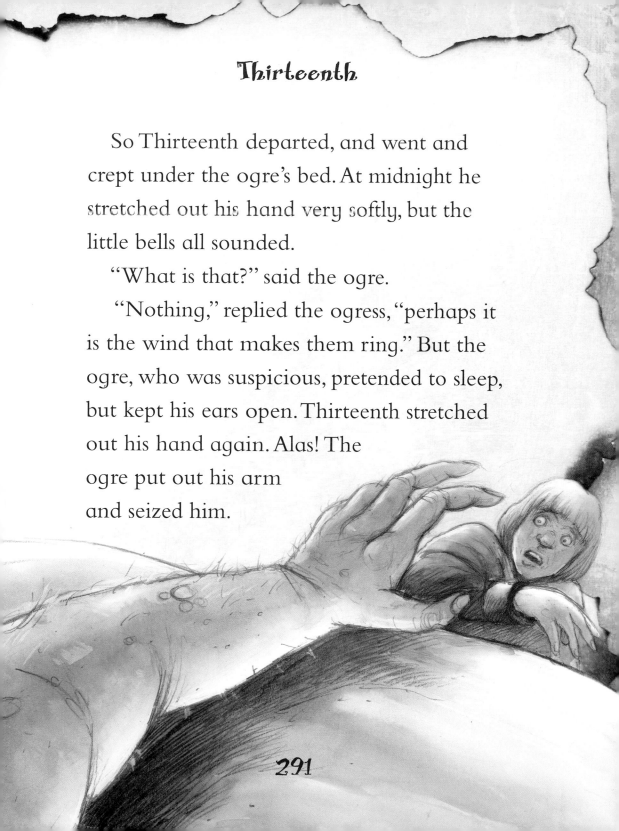

Thirteenth

So Thirteenth departed, and went and crept under the ogre's bed. At midnight he stretched out his hand very softly, but the little bells all sounded.

"What is that?" said the ogre.

"Nothing," replied the ogress, "perhaps it is the wind that makes them ring." But the ogre, who was suspicious, pretended to sleep, but kept his ears open. Thirteenth stretched out his hand again. Alas! The ogre put out his arm and seized him.

"Now you are caught! Just wait, I will have you for my supper." Then he put Thirteenth in a barrel. The ogre began to feed him on raisins and figs to get him fat enough to make a fine feast for him and his wife.

After a time, the ogre said, "Stick out your finger, little Thirteenth, so that I can see whether you are fat." Thirteenth saw a mouse's tail and stuck that out.

"Ah, how thin you are!" said the ogre. "And besides, you don't smell good! Eat, my son. Take the raisins and figs, and get fat soon!" After some days the ogre told him again to put out his finger and Thirteenth stuck out a splinter of wood. "Eh, wretch! Are you still so skinny? Eat, eat, and get fat soon."

Thirteenth

At the end of the month, Thirteenth had nothing more to stick out, and had to show his finger. The ogre cried out in joy, "He is fat, he is fat! Quick, my ogress, heat the oven for three nights and three days, for I am going to invite our relatives, and we will make a fine banquet of Thirteenth."

The ogress heated the oven for three days and three nights. Then she let Thirteenth out of the barrel, and said to him, "Come here, Thirteenth. You are going to help me put the lamb in the oven." But Thirteenth knew what she was planning, and when he approached the oven he said, "Ah, mother ogress, what is that black thing in the corner of the oven?" The ogress stooped down a little but saw nothing.

"Stoop down again," said Thirteenth, "so

that you can see it." When the ogress
stooped down again, Thirteenth seized her
by the feet and threw her into the oven. He
then closed the oven door and ran home.

After this, the King said to Thirteenth,
"Listen, Thirteenth. To complete your brave

tasks, I want you to bring me the ogre himself, in person, alive and well."

"How can I, Your Majesty?" said Thirteenth. But he thought awhile, then added, "I will have a try."

Thirteenth had a strong chest made, and disguised himself with a long, false beard. He went to the ogre's house and called out to him, "Do you know Thirteenth? The wretch! He has killed some of my brothers, but I'll catch him! And when I catch him, I will shut him up in this chest!"

At these words the ogre drew near and said, "I, too, would like to help you, for you don't know what he has done to me." And he began to tell his story.

The pretending old man said, "I do not know Thirteenth. Do you know him?"

"Yes, sir."

"Then tell me, how tall is he?"

"As tall as I am."

"If that is so," said Thirteenth, "let us see whether this chest will hold him. If it will hold you, it will hold him."

"Oh, good idea!" said the ogre, and he got into the chest. Then Thirteenth shut the chest and nailed it up, put it on a cart and went back to the city.

When he arrived, the King had an iron chain attached to the ogre's hands and feet, and made him gnaw bones for the rest of his miserable life. The King gave Thirteenth a huge pile of riches and treasures, and asked him always to stay by his side.

The Giant of the Flood

Gertrude Landa

Just before the world was drowned, all the animals gathered in front of the Ark and Father Noah carefully inspected them.

Then the various creatures began to march forwards into the Ark. Father Noah watched them closely. Something seemed to be troubling him.

"I wonder," he said, "how I can get a

297

unicorn, and how I shall get it into the Ark."

"I can bring you a unicorn," said a voice of thunder. Turning round, Noah saw the giant, Og. "But you must agree to save me, too, from the flood."

"Go away," cried Noah. "You are a demon, not a human being. I can have no dealings with you."

"Pity me," whined the giant. "Look how my figure is shrinking and shrinking. Once I was so tall that I could drink water from the clouds and toast fish at the sun. I'm not afraid that I shall be drowned, but that all the food will be destroyed and that I shall die of hunger."

Noah, however, only smiled. But he grew serious again when Og brought a unicorn. It was as big as a mountain, although the giant said that it was the smallest he could find.

For some time Noah was puzzled about what to do, but at last a bright idea struck him. He attached the huge unicorn to the Ark by a rope fastened to its horn, so that it could swim alongside and be fed.

Og seated himself on a mountain near at hand and watched the rain pouring down. Faster and faster it fell until the rivers overflowed and the waters began to rise rapidly on the land and sweep all things away.

Father Noah stood gloomily before the door of the Ark until the water reached his neck. Then it swept him inside. The door closed with a bang, and the Ark rose on the flood and began to move along. The

unicorn swam alongside, and as it passed
Og, the giant jumped on to its back!

"See, Father Noah," he cried, with a huge
chuckle, "you will have to save me after all.
I will snatch all the food you put through

the window for the unicorn."

Noah saw that it was useless to argue with Og, who might sink the Ark with his tremendous strength.

"I will make a bargain with you," Noah shouted from a window. "I will feed you, but you must promise to be a servant to my descendants."

Og was very hungry, so he accepted the conditions and devoured his first breakfast.

The rain continued to fall in great big sheets that shut out the light of day. However, inside the Ark all was bright and cheerful. Some of the animals were troublesome and Noah got no sleep at all. The lion had a bad attack of fever.

One day the rain stopped, the clouds rolled away and the sun shone brilliantly again. How strange the world looked! It was like a vast ocean. Nothing but water could be seen anywhere, and only one or two of the highest mountain tops peeped above the flood. All the world was drowned, and Noah gazed on the scene from one of the windows with tears in his eyes. Og, riding on the unicorn behind the Ark, was quite happy.

"Ha, ha!" he laughed. "I shall be able to eat and drink just as much as I like now and shall never be troubled by those tiny little creatures, the mortals."

"Be not so sure," said Noah. "Those tiny men and women shall be your masters and shall outlive you and the whole race of giants and demons."

The giant did not like that idea. He knew

that whatever Noah said would come true.
He was so sad that he ate no food for two
days, and began to grow smaller and
thinner. Og became more and more
unhappy as, day by day, the water went
down and the mountains began to appear.
At last the Ark rested on Mount Ararat, and
Og's long ride came to an end.

"I will soon leave you, Father Noah," he
said. "I shall wander round the world to see
what is left of it."

"You cannot go until I permit you," said
Noah. "Have you forgotten our agreement
so soon? You must be my servant. I have
work for you."

Giants are not fond of work, and Og,
who was the father of all the giants, was
lazy. He only wanted to eat and sleep, but

he knew he was in Noah's power, and he cried when he saw the land appear again.

"Stop," commanded Noah. "Do you want to drown the world all over again with your big tears?"

So Og sat on a mountain and rocked from side to side, crying silently to himself. He watched the animals leave the Ark and had to do all the hard work when Noah's children built houses. Daily he complained that he was shrinking to the size of a human, for Noah said there was not too much food.

One day Noah said to him, "Come with me, Og. I am going around the world to plant fruit and flowers to make the earth beautiful. I need your help."

For many days they wandered all over

the earth, and Og had to carry the heavy bag of seeds. The last thing Noah planted was the grapevine.

"What is this – food or drink?" asked Og.

"Both," replied Noah. "It can be eaten or its juice made into wine." As he planted it, he blessed the grape. "You shall be," he said, "a plant pleasing to the eye. Bear fruit that will be food for the hungry and a cheering drink to the thirsty."

Og himself often drank too much and many years afterward, when he was a servant to the patriarch Abraham, he was scolded until he became so frightened that one of his teeth dropped out. Abraham made an ivory chair for himself from this tooth. Afterwards Og became King of Bashan, but he forgot his agreement with

Noah. Instead of helping men, Og came to attack them. "I will kill them all with one blow," he declared.

Using all his enormous strength Og uprooted a mountain and, raising it high above his head, prepared to drop it on the people and crush them.

But a wonderful thing happened. The mountain was full of grasshoppers and ants who had bored millions of tiny holes in it. When King Og raised the great mass, it crumbled in his hands and fell over his head and round his neck like a collar. He tried to pull it off, but his teeth became tangled in the mass. As he danced about in rage and pain, Moses, the leader of the Israelites, approached him.

Moses was a tiny man compared with Og. With a mighty effort Moses jumped ten feet into the air and, raising his sword, he managed to strike the giant on the ankle and wound him.

And so, after many years, the terrible giant of the flood died because he broke his word to Father Noah.

WEIRD AND WONDERFUL BEASTS

John Malin and the
Bull-man   310

Perseus and the Gorgon   322

The Sphinx   334

The Bogey-Beast   340

The Red Ettin   349

The Master and his Pupil   359

The Cattle of Geryon   366

Talus, the Brass Giant   378

John Malin and the Bull-man

Katharine Pyle

A Louisiana tale

John Malin worked as a servant for a fine lady. The lady had a friend who was a handsome man with a fine, deep voice. The gentleman's name was Mr Bulbul. He often came to the house to take meals with the lady and he always spoke to John Malin very pleasantly. But John could not bear him.

Now, not far from the lady's house there

was a pasture, and in this pasture was a bull – a fine, handsome animal. John Malin often saw it there.

After a while, John began to notice that whenever Mr Bulbul came to the house, which was almost every day, the bull disappeared from the pasture. And whenever the bull was in the pasture, there was nothing to be seen of the gentleman.

"That is a curious thing," said John to himself. "I will watch and find out what this means. I am sure something is wrong."

So one day, John went out and hid himself behind some rocks at the edge of the pasture. The bull was grazing with its head down and did not see John. After a while the bull raised its head and looked all about to see if there was anyone around.

Then it dropped on its knees and cried,
"Beau Madjam, fat Madjam, djam, djam,
djara, djara!"

All of a sudden, the bull turned into a
man. The man was Mr Bulbul, who came
to visit John's mistress.

John Malin ran home to his mistress and
said, "Dear Mistress, Mr Bulbul is not a man
at all, but a bull monster. He uses magic to
make himself look like a man so as to come
to see you."

The lady began to laugh. "You are either
crazy or dreaming," she said. But John
Malin insisted that what he told her was
true. "I have seen it and I know it," he said.
"I will prove it to you."

After that, John went away by himself
and thought and thought. He tried to

remember the exact words the bull had said when he turned himself into a man, but he could not be sure what they were.

So the next day, John went out and hid himself behind the rocks again, taking care, as before, that the bull should not see him. The bull's head was down and it was eating grass.

However, it soon raised its head and looked all about. Seeing no one, the creature dropped on its knees and bellowed, "Beau Madjam, fat Madjam, djam, djam, djara, djara!"

All of a sudden, the bull became a man and walked away in the direction of the lady's house.

John Malin followed Mr Bulbul, saying over and over to himself quietly, "Beau

Madjam, fat Madjam, djam, djam, djara, djara. Beau Madjam, fat Madjam, djam, djam, djara, djara!"

When John Malin reached the house, Mr Bulbul was in the salon with his mistress. John could hear them talking together.

John Malin took a tray of cakes and wine and carried it into the salon, just as though his mistress had ordered him to do so. He went over to Mr Bulbul, so he was close in front of him, and then he said in a very low voice, as though just to himself, "Beau Madjam, fat Madjam, djam, djam, djara, djara!"

Such a noise you never heard. The fine Mr Bulbul bellowed aloud and jumped up, smashing his chair. The lady shrieked and almost fainted. Then, right there before

them, Mr Bulbul's head grew long and
hairy, horns sprouted from his forehead, his
arms turned into legs and his hands and
feet into hoofs, and he became a bull.

He galloped across the salon in a fright,
his hoofs clattering on the floor. The bull
burst out through the glass door so fast that
he carried it away on his horns and back
into the pasture with him.

John Malin and the Bull-man

Then the lady knew that everything John Malin had told her was true and she could not thank him enough.

John Malin was very happy, but he was sure the bull would try to revenge itself on him in some way or other. At last, John grew so afraid that he decided to go and talk to a wise man he knew who dealt in magic. John told him everything that had happened, then said, "And now, I am afraid, for I think he means to harm me."

"You do well to be afraid," said the wise man. "Bulbul will certainly try to do you harm. He knows much magic, but my magic is stronger than his and I will help you. Get me three owl's eggs and a cup of black goat's milk and bring them here."

John Malin went away and got the three

owl's eggs and the cup of black goat's milk, though they were not easy to find. Then he brought them to the wise man.

The wise man took them from him. He rolled the owl's eggs in the milk and made magic over them. Then he gave them back to John. "Keep these by you all the time," he said. "Then if the bull comes after you do thus and so, and this and the other, and you will have no more trouble with him."

John Malin thanked the wise man, gave him a piece of silver and went away with the eggs tied up in his handkerchief.

He had not gone more than halfway home, and was just coming out from a wood, when he heard a loud noise and the bull burst out of the trees and came charging towards him.

John Malin and the Bull-man

Quick as a flash, John Malin put the eggs in his mouth and climbed up a tree. The eggs were not broken.

The bull galloped up and struck the tree with its horns. "You think you are safe, but I will soon have you down," it cried.

Then the bull changed into a man. He had an axe in his hands and began to chop down the tree. *Gip, gop! Gip, gop!* The chips flew and the branches trembled.

John tried to remember the words that would turn the man back into a bull, but he was so frightened he could not think of them. What he did remember were the eggs that the man had given him. He took one out of his mouth and dropped it down on the bull-man's right shoulder. At once the bull-man's right arm fell off and the axe dropped to the ground. However, this did not trouble the bull-man. He picked up the axe with his left hand and chopped away, *Gip, gop! Gip, gop!* The chips flew faster than ever.

Then John Malin dropped the second egg down on the bull-man's left shoulder and his left arm fell off. Now the bull-man had no arms, but he took up the axe in his mouth and went on chopping, Gip, gop! Gip, gop! The whole tree shook and trembled.

Then John Malin dropped the third

and last egg down on the bull-man's head and at once his head fell off.

That ended the bull-man's magic. He could do nothing more and had to turn into a bull again. Away he galloped, with his tail in the air, and that was the last John Malin ever saw of him. What became of him nobody ever knew, but he must have gone far, far away.

John Malin climbed down from the tree and went home. After that, he lived very happily in the lady's house and was like a son to her.

Perseus and the Gorgon

James Baldwin

The Greek hero, Perseus, has been summoned
by his King, who has a task for him.

"The Gorgons," said the King, "are three terrible demon sisters who live in the middle of Africa. Their bodies are covered with dragon scales, their hands are claws, they have snakes instead of hair, and they have teeth as long as tusks. Whoever looks upon them is turned to stone. All three are dreadful, but the one who is named Medusa is the most dreadful of all. Now I have been thinking, as you are so fond of adventures, you will go and cut off Medusa's head."

Perseus was much too brave to refuse or even to think of refusing. So he lay down to get a little sleep before starting out.

He dreamt that Pluto, Minerva and Mercury came to his bedside and that each gave him a parting present. Pluto gave him a helmet, Minerva a shield and Mercury a pair of sandals, with little wings fastened to them. But the dream was not as strange as what he found when he woke up. There, on his bed, actually lay the helmet, the shield of polished steel and the winged sandals.

Well, somebody must have put them

there. So first Perseus put on the helmet, then he slung the shield over his shoulders, and last of all he put the winged sandals on his feet. When the wings spread themselves at his heels, and carried him high up into the air, he began to think that the visit from the gods must have been something more than a dream.

Perseus went up so high that the earth looked like a large map spread out below him. But not till nearly nightfall did he see, in the far distance, a cluster of palm trees. Reaching the palm trees at last, he found, in the midst of the cluster, a wooden hut.

He entered and found three very old women warming their hands at a few burning sticks. As he came in, the three crones turned their faces towards him.

Perseus and the Gorgon

Perseus saw that one of them had only one eye and no teeth, that another had only one tooth and no eye, and that the third had neither teeth nor eyes.

"I am a traveller," said Perseus, "and have lost my way. Will you kindly tell me where I am?"

"Come in and show yourself," said the crone who had the eye, sharply. "I must see who you are before I answer," she added, even though her one eye was looking straight at Perseus.

"Here I am," said Perseus, stepping into the middle of the room. "I suppose you can see me now."

"It's very strange – very strange!" said the old woman. "Sisters, I hear a man's voice but I see no man!"

"Nonsense, sister!" said the one who had the tooth. "You can't have put the eye in right. Let me try."

To the amazement of Perseus, the first old woman took out her eye and passed it to the second, who, after giving it a polish, put it into her own face and looked round. But she also saw nothing.

Perseus and the Gorgon

So they kept passing the eye round from one to another, and yet they could see nothing. At last Perseus, feeling terribly hot and tired, took off Pluto's helmet to cool himself, when suddenly –

"There he is! I see him now!" exclaimed the old woman who, at that moment, happened to be using the eye.

And so Perseus found out that his helmet made him invisible when he put it on.

He said, "Will you put me on the right road to where I want to go?"

It was the one who happened to have the eye in her head that always spoke.

"We are the three Grey Sisters. And where do you want to go?"

"I want to visit the Gorgons, particularly Medusa," said Perseus. "Do you happen to know where they are?"

"Of course we know! But never, no, never will we tell you where they live or the way to get there."

"Never!" croaked the old woman with the tooth.

"Never!" mumbled the third.

Perseus did all he could to persuade them, but they were so stubborn that he was only wasting words. Meanwhile, they laid out their supper, which they ate in a very strange way. They took turns with the one tooth that they had among them, and passed it round from one to the other, just as they did with their one eye. After supper, they put the eye and the tooth into a little box while they took a nap. Perseus, watching for his opportunity, snatched up the box, put on his helmet and cried out, "Now tell me the way to Medusa, or else you shall never see or eat again!"

The poor old Grey Sisters went down on their knees and begged him to give them back their only tooth and their only eye. But he said, "It is my turn to be stubborn. Tell me where to find Medusa."

"Very well," said the eldest Grey Sister, "you must go straight on, night and day, until you come into the country of King Atlas. Near the King's palace is a garden where the trees bear golden apples, guarded by a dragon. If the dragon does not devour you, you must pass the garden gate and go on, a long, long way, till you come to a great lake where, if you do not find the Gorgons, you will be a lucky man."

WEIRD AND WONDERFUL BEASTS

Perseus gave the old women back their tooth and eye, which they received with joy, left the hut and travelled on. After many days he came into a fertile country where he found a great garden enclosed by a high wall, and sure enough, at the gate sat a monstrous dragon with glaring eyes. But Perseus, wearing his invisible helmet, passed by safely.

In time he came to the lake, where he took off his helmet to quench his thirst. While he was drinking, Perseus was startled by the approach of what sounded like a mighty rush of wind. He had just enough time to put his helmet on again before he saw, reflected in the lake, the flying form of the terrible Medusa – the Gorgon – whom he had vowed to slay.

Perseus and the Gorgon

Medusa, not seeing Perseus, sat down beside him with folded wings.

Perseus remembered what would happen to him if he looked at Medusa. And yet how in the world was he to fight her without looking at her? Suddenly he thought of Minerva's shield, which was polished like a mirror. He turned it towards Medusa and saw not herself, but her reflection in the polished shield, which did just as well.

She was indeed a monster – even more terrible than Perseus had expected. Medusa was of gigantic size, hideous and cruel in face, with the scales and wings of a dragon, horrible claws, and hundreds of writhing and hissing snakes on her head instead of hair. No wonder that anyone who looked on her was turned into stone straight away.

Perseus, wearing his helmet and guiding himself by his mirror, from which he never moved his eyes, drew his blade and sprang upon the monster. He gave one stroke just between her chin and where her scales began, and, in a single moment, her hideous head was rolling on the sand. The snakes gave one last hiss, and the deed was done.

Still keeping his eyes turned away, Perseus, using his shield as a mirror, found Medusa's head. He slung it out of his sight behind him. Then, rising into the air, Perseus flew homewards.

The Sphinx

Anon

Many, many years ago, there was a terrible monster that haunted the land of Egypt. It was called the Sphinx, and it caused terror to the lands around the city of Thebes. The Sphinx had the body of a strong, powerful lion, with sharp claws covered in dried blood. Its head was that of a woman – not a gentle, smiling woman, but a terrible, cruel-faced woman.

The Sphinx

She lurked on the road into the town of Thebes, and all travellers had to pass her to continue along the road. For on one side there was a high cliff that no one could climb, and on the other a terrible precipice that fell down, down, down to a rocky river far below. Every time a traveller passed the Sphinx, she caught them, and told them that she would only let them go if they could answer her question.

"What animal is it that goes on four feet in the morning, on two feet at noon, and on three legs in the evening?" the Sphinx would ask, and her lips would curve in a smile.

No one could answer the question and she would throw them over the precipice. There wasn't anyone that could defeat her because no one could guess the riddle.

The Sphinx

One day, the Greek Oedipus came travelling towards the city of Thebes. The Sphinx crouched face to face with him and spoke the riddle that none had been able to guess.

"What animal is it that in the morning goes on four feet, at noon on two feet, and in the evening on three legs?"

Oedipus, hiding his dread of the terrible creature, sat on the sand and thought carefully. Then he answered, "Man. In childhood he crawls on hands and knees, as a grown-up he walks upright on two legs, but in old age he needs a stick to help him."

At this reply the Sphinx uttered a cry, sprang from the rock into the valley below, and died where she had thrown so many people before her. Oedipus had guessed the answer correctly.

When Oedipus came to the city and told the people of Thebes that the Sphinx was gone, they greeted him as their rescuer. They took Oedipus to the best house in the town and begged him to rest while they washed his feet and combed his hair. Then they brought a feast of cheese, tender young lamb, grapes, bread and honey, with tall jugs of red wine. They invited Oedipus to rest, eat and drink while they sang songs in his praise. The evil monster would trouble them no more and they could walk their roads in peace at last.

The Bogey-Beast

Flora Annie Steel

There was once a woman who was very cheerful, though she had little to make her so. She was poor and lonely. The woman lived in a little cottage and earned a small living by running errands for her neighbours, getting a bite here and a sup there, as reward for her services. She always looked as lively and cheery as if she had not a want in the world.

The Bogey-Beast

Now, one summer evening, as the woman was walking along the high road to her cottage, full of smiles as ever, she saw a big black pot lying in the ditch.

"Goodness me!" she cried, "That would be just the very thing for me if I only had something to put in it. But I haven't. Now who could have left it in the ditch?"

She looked about her expecting the owner would not be far off, but she could see nobody.

"Maybe there is a hole in it," she went on, "and that's why it has been cast away. But it would do fine to put a flower in for my window, so I'll take it home with me."

And with that she lifted the lid and looked inside. "Mercy me!" she cried. "If it isn't full of gold pieces. Here's luck!"

And so it was, full of great gold coins.
Well, at first the woman simply stood still,
wondering if she was standing on her head
or her heels. Then she began saying to
herself, "Crikey! But I do feel rich. I feel
awfully rich!"

After she had said this many times, she
began to wonder how she was going to
get her treasure home. It was too heavy for
her to carry. She could see no better way
than to tie the end of her shawl to the pot
and drag it behind her.

"It will soon be dark," she said to herself
as she walked along. "So much the better!
The neighbours will not see what I'm
bringing home. I shall have all night to
myself and will be able to think about what
to do! Maybe I'll buy a grand house and

just sit by the fire with a cup of tea and do no work at all like a queen. Or maybe I'll bury it at the bottom of the garden and just keep a bit in the old china teapot. Or maybe – Goody! Goody! I feel that grand I don't know myself!"

By this time she was a bit tired of dragging such a heavy weight and, stopping to rest a while, she turned to look at the treasure behind her.

It wasn't a pot of gold at all! It was nothing but a lump of silver.

The woman stared at it, rubbed her eyes and stared at it again. "Well! I never!" she said at last. "And me thinking it was a pot of gold! I must have been dreaming. But this is luck! Silver is far less trouble – easier to mind and not so easily stolen. Those gold pieces would have been the death of me, and with this great lump of silver – "

So she went off again, planning what she would do and feeling very rich. Becoming a bit tired again, she stopped to rest and looked around to see if her treasure was safe. But she saw nothing but a great lump of iron!

"Well! I never!" she said again. "And I mistook it for silver! I must have been dreaming. But this is luck! It's really convenient. I can get penny pieces for old iron, and penny pieces are a great deal handier for me than gold and silver. Why! I should never have slept a wink for fear of being robbed. But a penny piece comes in useful, and I shall sell that iron for a lot and be rich – rolling rich."

So on she walked, full of plans as to how she would spend her penny pieces. Once more she stopped to rest and looked round to see if her treasure was safe. And this time she saw nothing but a big stone!

"Well! I never!" she cried, full of smiles. "And to think I mistook it for iron. I must have been dreaming. But here's luck indeed, with me badly wanting a stone to stick open the gate. It's a change for the better! It's a fine thing to have good luck."

So, all in a hurry to see how the stone would keep the gate open, the woman walked off down the hill till she came to her own cottage. She unlatched the gate and then turned to unfasten her shawl from the stone, which lay on the path behind her. It was a stone sure enough. There was plenty of light to see it lying there, sweet and peaceful as a stone should.

So the woman bent over the stone to unfasten the shawl end, when –

"Oh my!"

All of a sudden the stone gave a jump, a squeal, and in one moment it was as big as a haystack. Then it let down four great, lanky legs and threw out two long ears, flourished a great long tail, and romped off, kicking and squealing and whinnying and laughing like a naughty, mischievous boy!

The woman stared after the creature till it was nearly out of sight, and then she burst out laughing.

"Well!" she chuckled, "I am in luck! Quite the luckiest body hereabouts. Fancy my seeing the Bogey-Beast all to myself!

The Bogey-Beast

And making myself so free with it too! My goodness! I do feel uplifted – that grand!"

So she went into her cottage and spent the evening chuckling over her good luck.

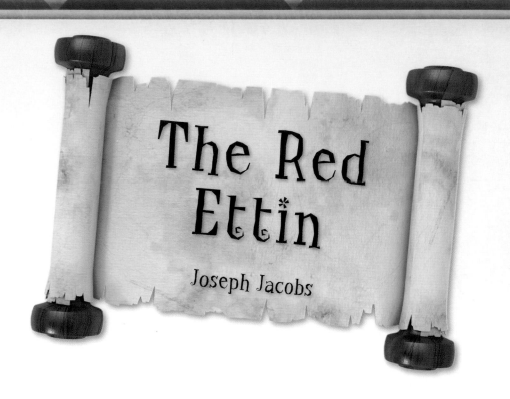

The Red Ettin

Joseph Jacobs

There was once a widow who lived on a small bit of ground, which she rented from a farmer. She had two sons, and it was time for the widow to send them away to seek their fortunes.

So the oldest young man went to seek his fortune first. And he went all that day and all the next day. On the third day, in the afternoon, he came up to where a shepherd

349

was sitting with a flock of sheep. He went up to the shepherd and asked him who the sheep belonged to. The shepherd answered, "The Red Ettin of Ireland."

The shepherd also told the young man to beware of the beasts he should meet next, for they were of a very different kind from any he had yet seen.

So the young man went on, and he saw very dreadful beasts with two heads, and on every head four horns. He was frightened and ran away from them as fast as he could.

The young man was glad when he came to a castle that stood on a small hill, with the door standing wide open to the wall. He went into the castle for shelter, and saw an old woman sitting beside the kitchen fire.

The Red Ettin

He asked her if he might stay for the night, as he was tired from a long journey. The old woman said he might, but that the castle was not a good place for him to be in. It belonged to the Red Ettin, a terrible beast with three heads, who spared no living man it could get hold of.

The young man would have gone away, but he was afraid of the beasts outside of the castle. He begged the old woman to hide him as best she could, and not tell the Red Ettin he was there. He thought if he could last the night, he might get away in the morning without meeting with the beasts, and so escape.

But he had not been long in his hiding place before the awful Red Ettin came in. And no sooner was he in, than he cried out:

"Snouk but and snouk ben,
  I find the smell of an earthly man.
  Be he living, or be he dead,
  His heart this night shall kitchen
    my bread."

The monster soon found the poor young man and pulled him from his hole. He then told him that if he could answer three questions, his life would be spared.

So the first of the Red Ettin's heads asked, "A thing without an end, what's that?" But the young man knew not. Then the second head said, "The smaller, the more dangerous, what's that?" But the young man knew not. And then the third head asked, "When does the dead carry the living, riddle me that?" But the young man knew not and had to give up.

The Red Ettin

He was unable to answer one of these questions, and the Red Ettin took a mallet and knocked him on the head, and turned him into a pillar of stone.

The morning after, the younger brother told his mother that the time had now come for him to go upon his travels also. After he had travelled far, he met with an old woman who asked him if he would give her a bit of his bread. He said, "I will gladly do that." For the bread she gave him a magical wand that might be of service to him, if he took care to use it rightly.

He went on a great way farther, and then he came to the shepherd. When he asked whose sheep they were, the answer was, "The Red Ettin of Ireland."

When he came to the place where the

monstrous beasts were standing, he did not stop nor run away, but went boldly through them. One came up, roaring with an open mouth to devour him, but when he struck it with his wand, it was in an instant dead at his feet.

He soon came to the Red Ettin's castle, where he knocked and was admitted. The old woman by the fire warned the young man of the terrible Red Ettin, and what had been the fate of his brother. But he was not to be daunted. The monster soon came in, saying:

"Snouk but and snouk ben,
   I find the smell of an earthly man.
   Be he living, or be he dead,
   His heart shall be kitchen to
      my bread."

He quickly caught sight of the young man and bade him come forth on the floor. And then he put the three questions to him. But the young man had been told everything by the good fairy, so he was able to answer all the questions.

When the first head asked, "What's a thing without an end?" he said, "A bowl." And when the second head said, "The smaller, the more dangerous, what's that?" he said at once, "A bridge." And last, the third head said, "When does the dead carry the living, riddle me that?" The young man answered at once and said, "When a ship sails on the sea with men inside her." When the Red Ettin heard this, he knew that his power was gone. The young man took up an axe and cut off the monster's three heads.

The Red Ettin

The old woman took him upstairs and opened a great many doors. Out of every door came a beautiful lady who had been imprisoned there by the Red Ettin, and one of the ladies was the King's daughter. The old woman took the young man down into a low room, and there stood a stone pillar. He pointed his wand at it and his brother started to life.

All the prisoners were overjoyed at their rescue, for which they thanked the young man. The next day they all set out for the King's court. The King married his daughter to the young man who had rescued her and gave a noble's daughter to his brother. And so they all lived happily for the rest of their days.

The Master and his Pupil

Joseph Jacobs

There was once a very clever man in the north country who knew all the languages under the sun. He had one big book bound in black calf skin and clasped with iron, and with iron corners. It was chained to a table, which was fastened to the floor. When he read out of this book, he unlocked it with an iron key, and no one but he read from it, for it contained all the secrets of the world. It told how many angels there were in heaven. And it told of the demons, how many of them there were, what their powers and names were, and how they might be summoned and chained to be slaves to man.

The master had a pupil who was a foolish lad. He was never allowed to look into the black book or to enter the private room.

One day, when the master was out, the lad, as curious as could be, hurried to the private room. This was where his master kept his equipment for changing copper into gold and lead into silver. And where was his mirror, in which he could see all that was passing in the world. And where was the shell, which, when held to the ear, whispered all the words that were being spoken by anyone the master wanted to know about.

The lad tried in vain to turn copper and lead into gold and silver. He looked long into the mirror – smoke and clouds passed over it, but he saw nothing clear. And the shell to his ear produced only indistinct murmurings, like the breaking of distant seas on an unknown shore. "I can do nothing," he said, "as I don't know the right words to utter, and they are locked up in the magic book."

He looked round and saw the book was unfastened – the master had forgotten to lock it before he went out. The lad rushed to it and opened the book. It was written with red and black ink, and much of it he could not understand. But he put his finger on a line and read it through.

At once the room became dark and the house trembled. A clap of thunder rolled through the passage and the old room. And there stood before the lad a horrible monster, breathing fire and with eyes like burning lamps. It was the demon Beelzebub, whom he had called up to serve him.

"Set me a task!" said he, with a voice like the roaring of an iron furnace.

The lad only trembled and his hair stood up on his head.

"Set me a task!"

But the lad could not speak. Then the monster stepped towards him and, putting forth his hands, touched the lad's throat. The fingers burned his flesh. "Set me a task!"

"Water the flower!" cried the lad in

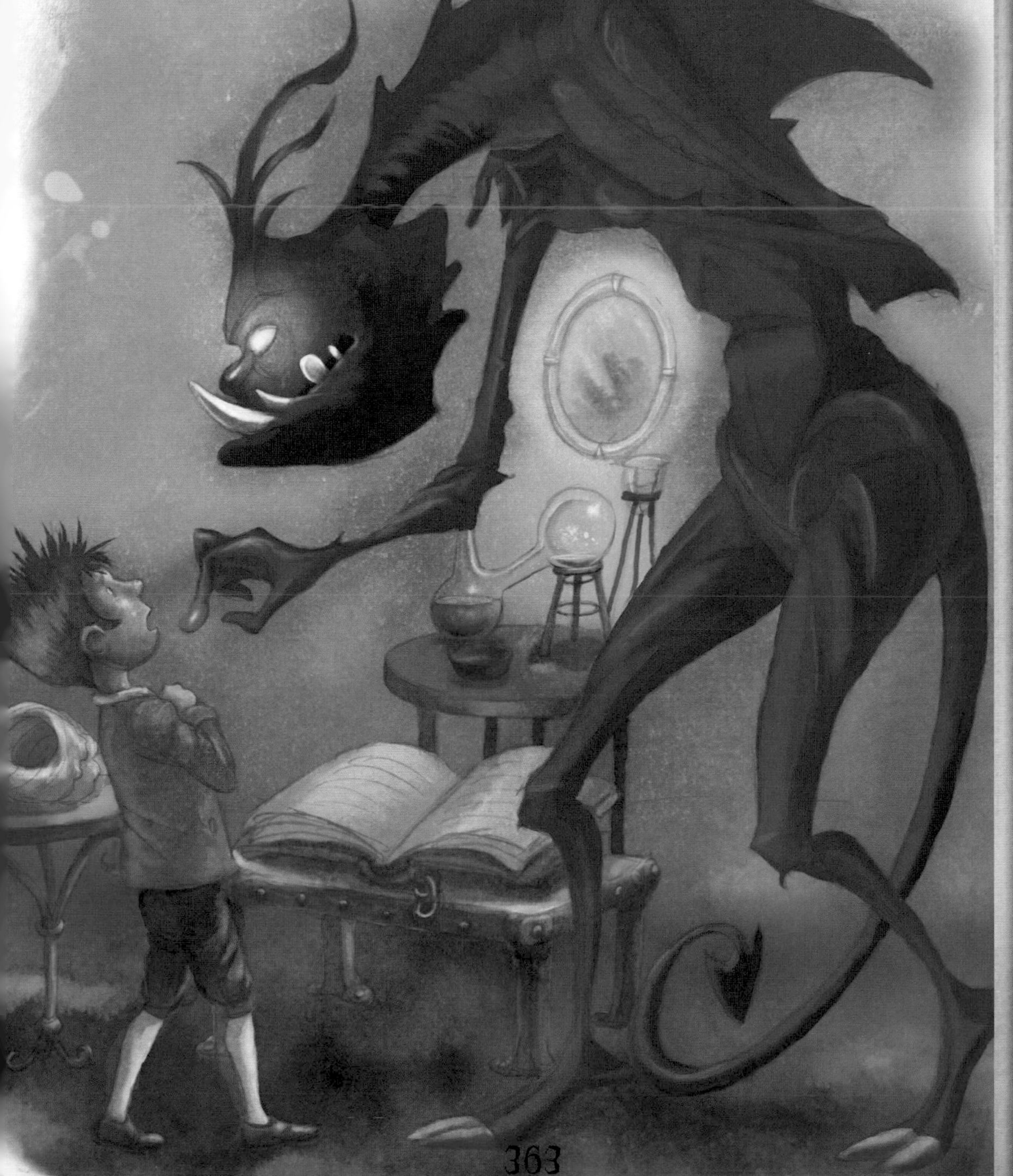

The Master and his Pupil

despair, pointing to a geranium that stood
in a pot on the floor. Instantly the monster
left the room, but in another instant he
returned with a barrel on his back. He
poured its contents over the flower. And
again and again he went and came,
pouring more and more water, till it was
ankle-deep on the floor of the room.

"Enough, enough!" gasped the lad. But
the monster took no notice. The lad didn't
know the words by which to send him
away, and still he fetched water.

It rose to the lad's knees and still more
water was poured. It rose to his waist, and
Beelzebub still kept on bringing barrels full.
It rose to his armpits and he scrambled on
top of the table. And now the water in the
room stood up to the window and washed

against the glass, and swirled around the lad's feet on the table. It still rose — it reached his chest. In vain he cried, but the monster would not be dismissed.

To this day, Beelzebub would have been pouring water, and would have drowned all Yorkshire. But the master remembered on his journey that he had not locked his book and came back. At the moment when the water was bubbling about the pupil's chin, the master rushed into the room and spoke the words that cast Beelzebub back into his fiery home.

And the master never left his book unlocked again.

The Cattle of Geryon

R E Francillon
From *Of Gods and Monsters*

The great Greek hero, Hercules, has been set a series of tasks by his cousin, King Eurystheus. Every time Eurystheus comes up with a task that he thinks is impossible, Hercules manages to complete it.

Eurystheus was at his wits' end coming up with work for his cousin. 'I must send Hercules to the very end of the earth,' thought Eurystheus. So he talked with every traveller who came to Mycenae, and in time had the good luck to hear of a suitable monster named Geryon, who lived in a cave at Gades, on the coast of Spain. This was very near indeed to what the Greeks then thought to be the end of the world.

Geryon, so the travellers reported, had three bodies and three heads, and kept large and valuable flocks and herds. 'That will be just the thing for Hercules!' thought Eurystheus. So he called Hercules and said, "Go to Gades and get me the cattle and the sheep of Geryon."

So Hercules set off for Spain by way of Egypt and the great Libyan desert.

He travelled on until one day he reached a pile of human skulls, nearly as big as a mountain. While wondering at the sight, a shadow fell over him and a big voice said,

"Yes, you may well look at that! I have nearly enough now."

It was a giant, nearly as high as the pile of skulls. "And who are you?" asked Hercules, "And what are these?"

"I am Antaeus," answered the giant, "the Sea is my father and the Earth is my mother. I am collecting skulls in order to build a temple with them, upon my mother the Earth, to my father the Sea."

"And how," asked Hercules, "have you managed to get so many?"

The Cattle of Geryon

"By killing everybody I see and adding his skull to the heap – as I am going to add yours."

So saying, he seized Hercules to kill him. But he was amazed to find that he himself was dashed to the ground, with force enough to break any ordinary bones. However, Antaeus, though astonished, was not in the least hurt, so it was the turn of Hercules to be surprised. Again they grabbed at each other, and again Hercules threw the giant, with still greater strength. Again and again Hercules threw him, but every time with greater difficulty. The more he was thrown, the stronger the giant became – he rose from every fall fresher than before. If this went on, Antaeus would become stronger than Hercules and would end by winning.

Now, Hercules thought it seemed very strange that each time the giant was dashed to the ground, the fresher and stronger he should grow.

'I see!' thought Hercules to himself. 'This giant is the son of the Earth, so whenever he falls, he is falling upon his own mother, who strengthens and refreshes her son. I must find another way.'

So thinking, Hercules put out all his strength and lifted Antaeus in his arms. But this time he did not dash him to the Earth –

370

he held him in the air and crushed him to death between his hands.

After this, Hercules travelled on without further adventure, until he reached the far western end of the Mediterranean Sea, which was thought to be the end of the world. It is where the south of Spain nearly touches Africa.

To get from there to Gades was no great distance. And to kill the monster Geryon, and to seize his flocks and herds for Eurystheus, was not very hard after what he had already done. But to drive such a number of sheep and cattle all the way from Gades in Spain to Mycenae in Greece was not an easy matter.

There was only one way of doing so without being stopped somewhere along the way by the sea, and this was by crossing two great mountain ranges – the Pyrenees and the Alps.

For one man to drive thousands of sheep and thousands of horned cattle over such mountains as those was the most tiresome and troublesome labour that Hercules had ever undergone.

He got as far as Italy without the loss of a single sheep or cow, and thought that he had seen the end of his trouble.

However, one morning, having counted the sheep and cattle as usual, and having gone some miles upon his day's journey, Hercules became aware that there was something wrong.

The sheep began to bleat and the cattle to bellow in an odd and excited way. And frequently, from behind him, Hercules heard an answering sound that at first he took for an echo. But no, it could not be that, for an echo would have repeated the bleating as well as the bellowing. And what Hercules heard behind him was the sound of bellowing only – precisely like that of Geryon's cows.

Hercules counted the flocks and herds over again and, though he was convinced that it was all right at the start, he found a full dozen missing.

Now a dozen was not much to lose out of thousands. But Hercules had been ordered to bring back all of the herds and flocks, and he would have felt that he had not done his duty if he lost even one lamb on the way.

So, following the distant sound, Hercules drove his sheep and cattle back across the hills, league after league, till he reached a huge, black cavern, the mouth of which was heaped with human bones.

His cattle became more excited and more difficult to control, for the sound Hercules was following came from within this huge cave.

Hercules was about to enter the cave and search it, when a three-headed ogre came out. The ogre's three mouths, when he opened them to speak, breathed smoke and flames.

"This is my cave," said he, with all three mouths at once, "and no man shall enter it but I."

"I only want my cattle," said Hercules.

The Cattle of Geryon

"Bring them out to me."

"Cattle?" asked the ogre. "There are no cattle here. I swear it by the head of my own mother."

"And who was she," asked Hercules, "that her head is an oath to swear by?"

"I am Cacus, the son of the Gorgon Medusa," answered the ogre, "I swear—"

But before he could finish, there came such a bellowing from within the cave that the very cattle seemed as if they were saying that Cacus lied.

"I am sorry," said Hercules. "I am weary of travelling, and of monsters, and of giants, and of ogres, and of liars, and of thieves. I really do not want to kill anymore. You are not one of my labours and I have had enough trouble."

Cacus laughed. "Do you see those bones?" he asked. "They are all that is left of people who have looked for what they have lost in my cave."

"Then," said Hercules, "either you shall add mine to the heap or I will add yours."

The Cattle of Geryon

And presently the bones of Cacus the Robber were added to the heap and Hercules, having got his cattle back, at last reached Mycenae.

Talus, the Brass Giant

Charles Kingsley
From *The Heroes*

This is part of the story of Jason and the Argonauts. Jason and his warriors are travelling back to his home with the sorceress Medea, when they come to the island of Talus.

They rowed for many a weary day until their water was drunk and their food was eaten. But last they saw a long, steep island ahead.

"We will land here," they cried, "and fill our water casks upon the shore."

But when they came nearer to the island, they saw a wondrous sight. For on the cliffs stood a giant, taller than any mountain.

When the giant saw the ship Argo and her crew he came towards them, more swiftly than the swiftest horse, and he shouted to them, "You are pirates, you are robbers! If you land here, you shall die."

Then the heroes pulled on their oars in fear, but Medea spoke, "I know this giant. If strangers land, he leaps into his furnace, which flames there among the hills. And when he is red-hot, he rushes on them and burns them in his brass hands. But he has only one vein in all his body, filled with liquid fire, and this vein is closed with a nail. I will find out where the nail is placed, and when I have got it in my hands, you shall

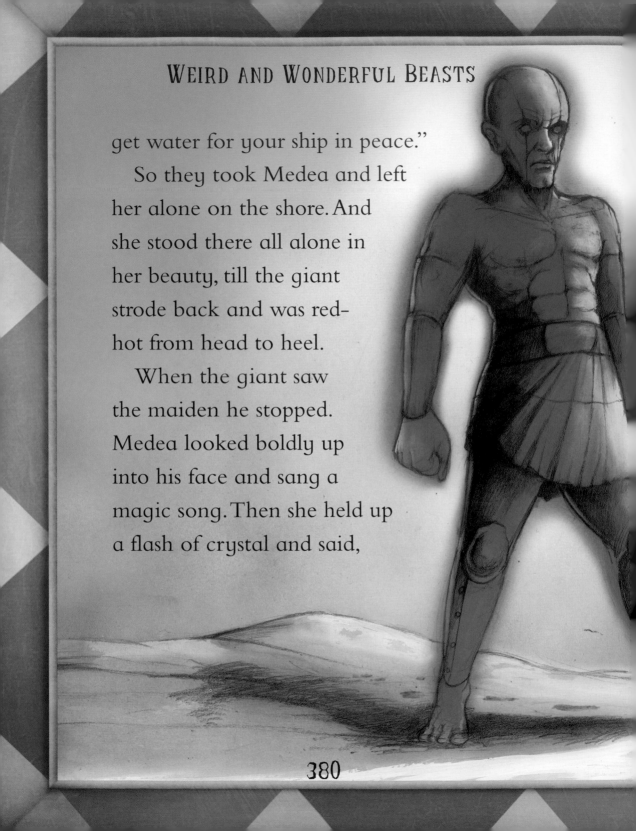

get water for your ship in peace."

So they took Medea and left her alone on the shore. And she stood there all alone in her beauty, till the giant strode back and was red-hot from head to heel.

When the giant saw the maiden he stopped. Medea looked boldly up into his face and sang a magic song. Then she held up a flash of crystal and said,

Talus, the Brass Giant

"I am Medea, the sorceress. My sister, Circe, gave me this and said, 'Go, reward Talus, the faithful giant, for his fame has gone out into all lands.' So I have come and I will pour this into your vein, so that you may live forever."

Talus listened to her false words and came near.

Medea said, "Dip yourself in the sea first to cool yourself, in case you burn my tender hands. Then show me the nail in your vein, and in that I will pour the liquid from the crystal flask."

Then Talus dipped himself, hissing, in the sea and then knelt before Medea and showed her the secret nail.

Medea drew the nail out gently, but she poured nothing in, and instead the liquid fire streamed forth.

Talus, the Brass Giant

Talus tried to leap up, crying, "You have betrayed me, false witch-maiden."

But Medea lifted up her hands before him and sang, till he sank beneath her spell.

And as Talus sank, the earth groaned beneath his weight and the liquid fire ran from his heel, like a stream of lava, down to the sea.

Then Medea laughed and called to the heroes, "Come and get water for your ship in peace."

So they came and found the giant lying dead. They fell down and kissed Medea's feet, watered their ship, took sheep and oxen, and so left that unfriendly shore.

And at last, after many weary days and nights, all worn and tired, the heroes saw once more their home, Iolcos, by the sea.